Algernon Blackwood's
THE Willows

ALGERNON BLACKWOOD'S THE WILLOWS

Entire contents copyright © 2019 by Nathan Carson and Sam Ford.
All rights reserved.
Based on the novella *The Willows* by Algernon Blackwood.
No part of this book (except small portions for review purposes) may be reproduced
in any form without written permission from Nathan Carson, Sam Ford or Floating World Comics.

Floating World Comics
400 NW Couch St.
Portland, OR 97209
www.floatingworldcomics.com

First paperback edition: October 2019
Printed in China.

ISBN 978-1-942801-75-7

Written by
NATHAN CARSON

Artwork by
SAM FORD

Based on the Novella by
ALGERNON BLACKWOOD

Lettered by
JASON FISCHER

Edited by
JASON LEIVIAN

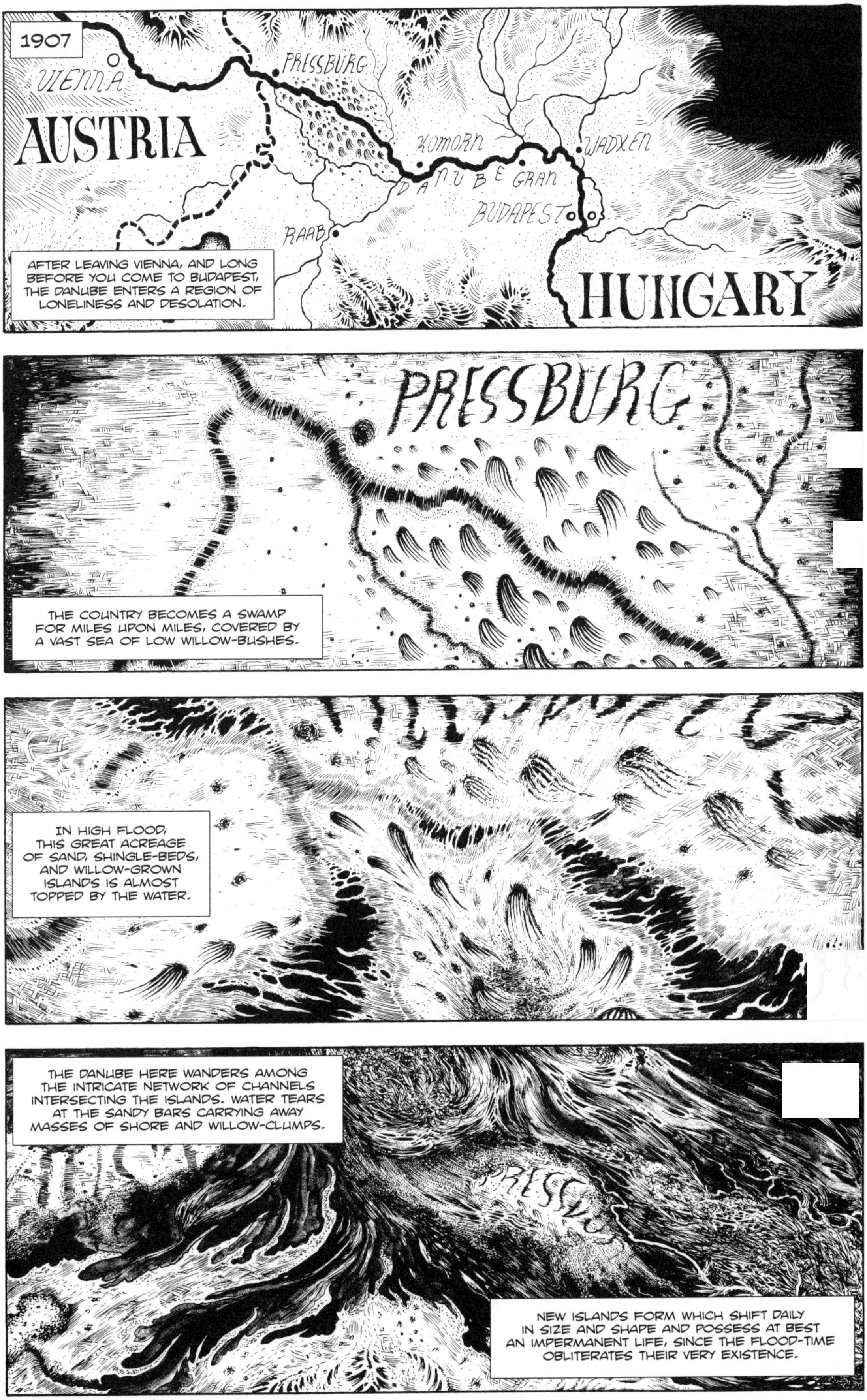
1907
VIENNA
AUSTRIA
PRESSBURG
KOMORN
WADXEN
DANUBE
GRAN
BUDAPEST
RAAB
HUNGARY
AFTER LEAVING VIENNA, AND LONG BEFORE YOU COME TO BUDAPEST, THE DANUBE ENTERS A REGION OF LONELINESS AND DESOLATION.
PRESSBURG
THE COUNTRY BECOMES A SWAMP FOR MILES UPON MILES, COVERED BY A VAST SEA OF LOW WILLOW-BUSHES.
IN HIGH FLOOD, THIS GREAT ACREAGE OF SAND, SHINGLE-BEDS, AND WILLOW-GROWN ISLANDS IS ALMOST TOPPED BY THE WATER.
THE DANUBE HERE WANDERS AMONG THE INTRICATE NETWORK OF CHANNELS INTERSECTING THE ISLANDS. WATER TEARS AT THE SANDY BARS CARRYING AWAY MASSES OF SHORE AND WILLOW-CLUMPS.
NEW ISLANDS FORM WHICH SHIFT DAILY IN SIZE AND SHAPE AND POSSESS AT BEST AN IMPERMANENT LIFE, SINCE THE FLOOD-TIME OBLITERATES THEIR VERY EXISTENCE.

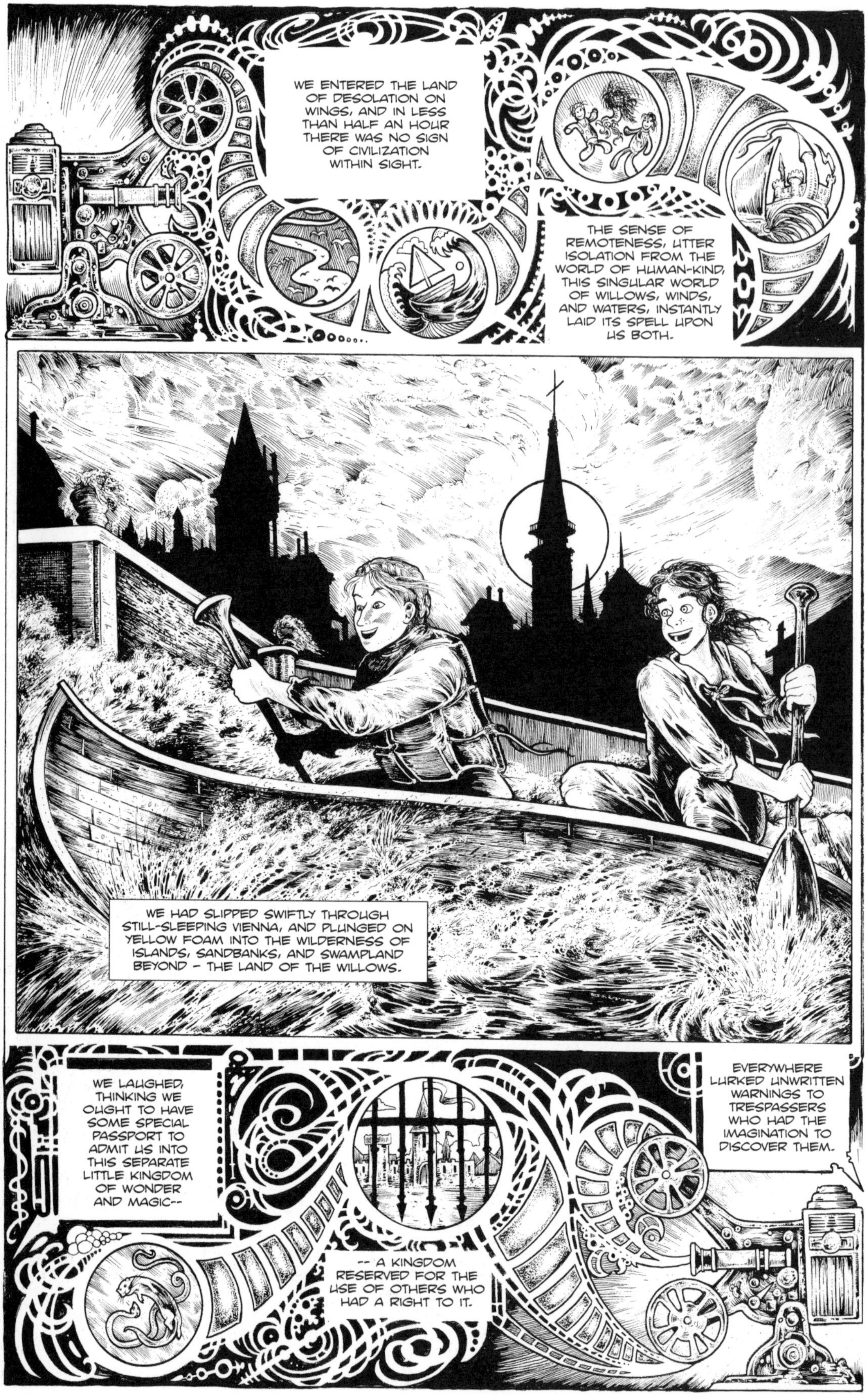

WE ENTERED THE LAND OF DESOLATION ON WINGS, AND IN LESS THAN HALF AN HOUR THERE WAS NO SIGN OF CIVILIZATION WITHIN SIGHT.
THE SENSE OF REMOTENESS, UTTER ISOLATION FROM THE WORLD OF HUMAN-KIND, THIS SINGULAR WORLD OF WILLOWS, WINDS, AND WATERS, INSTANTLY LAID ITS SPELL UPON US BOTH.
WE HAD SLIPPED SWIFTLY THROUGH STILL-SLEEPING VIENNA, AND PLUNGED ON YELLOW FOAM INTO THE WILDERNESS OF ISLANDS, SANDBANKS, AND SWAMPLAND BEYOND – THE LAND OF THE WILLOWS.
WE LAUGHED, THINKING WE OUGHT TO HAVE SOME SPECIAL PASSPORT TO ADMIT US INTO THIS SEPARATE LITTLE KINGDOM OF WONDER AND MAGIC--
-- A KINGDOM RESERVED FOR THE USE OF OTHERS WHO HAD A RIGHT TO IT.
EVERYWHERE LURKED UNWRITTEN WARNINGS TO TRESPASSERS WHO HAD THE IMAGINATION TO DISCOVER THEM.

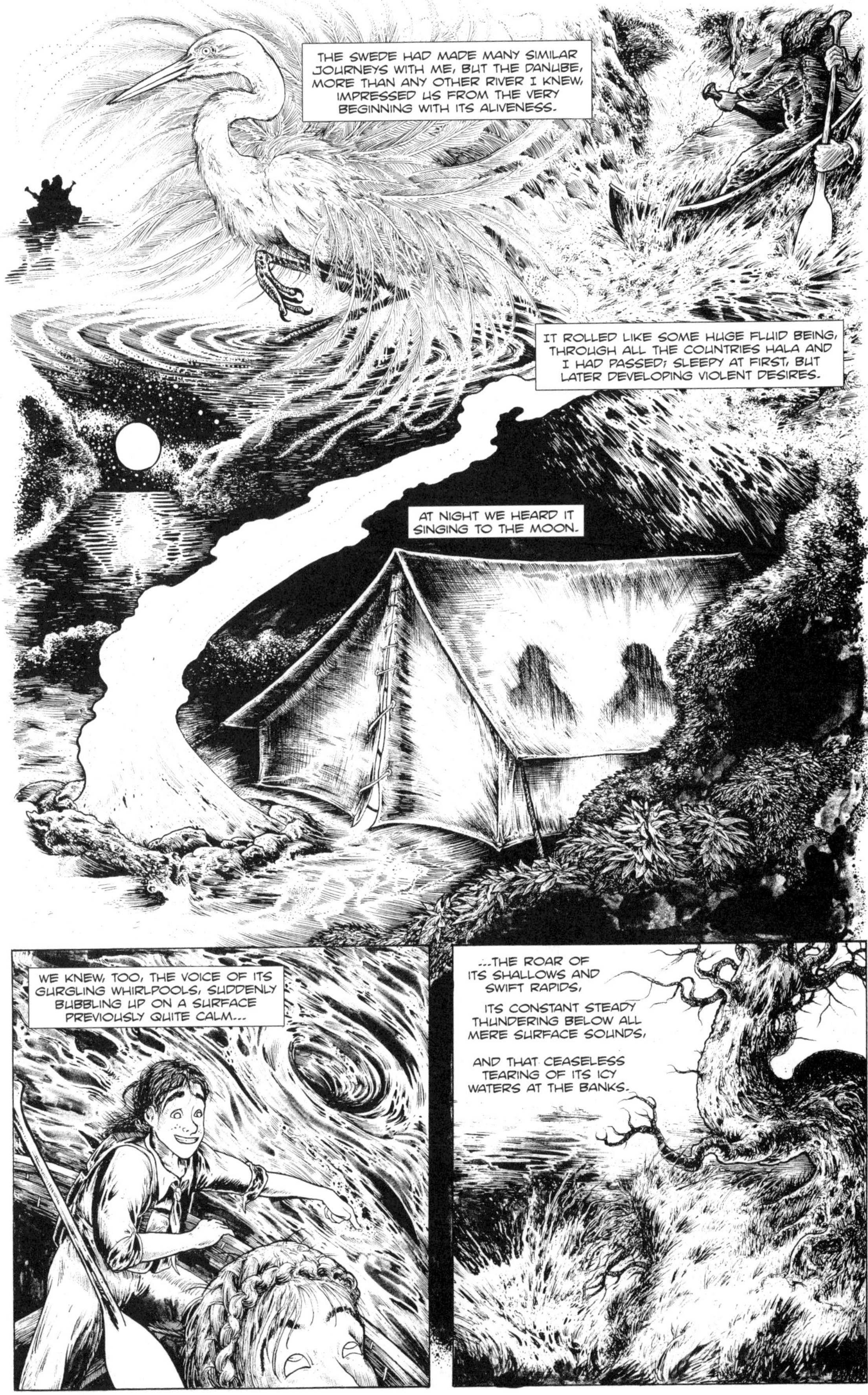
THE SWEDE HAD MADE MANY SIMILAR JOURNEYS WITH ME, BUT THE DANUBE, MORE THAN ANY OTHER RIVER I KNEW, IMPRESSED US FROM THE VERY BEGINNING WITH ITS ALIVENESS.
IT ROLLED LIKE SOME HUGE FLUID BEING, THROUGH ALL THE COUNTRIES HALA AND I HAD PASSED; SLEEPY AT FIRST, BUT LATER DEVELOPING VIOLENT DESIRES.
AT NIGHT WE HEARD IT SINGING TO THE MOON.
WE KNEW, TOO, THE VOICE OF ITS GURGLING WHIRLPOOLS, SUDDENLY BUBBLING UP ON A SURFACE PREVIOUSLY QUITE CALM...
...THE ROAR OF ITS SHALLOWS AND SWIFT RAPIDS,
ITS CONSTANT STEADY THUNDERING BELOW ALL MERE SURFACE SOUNDS,
AND THAT CEASELESS TEARING OF ITS ICY WATERS AT THE BANKS.

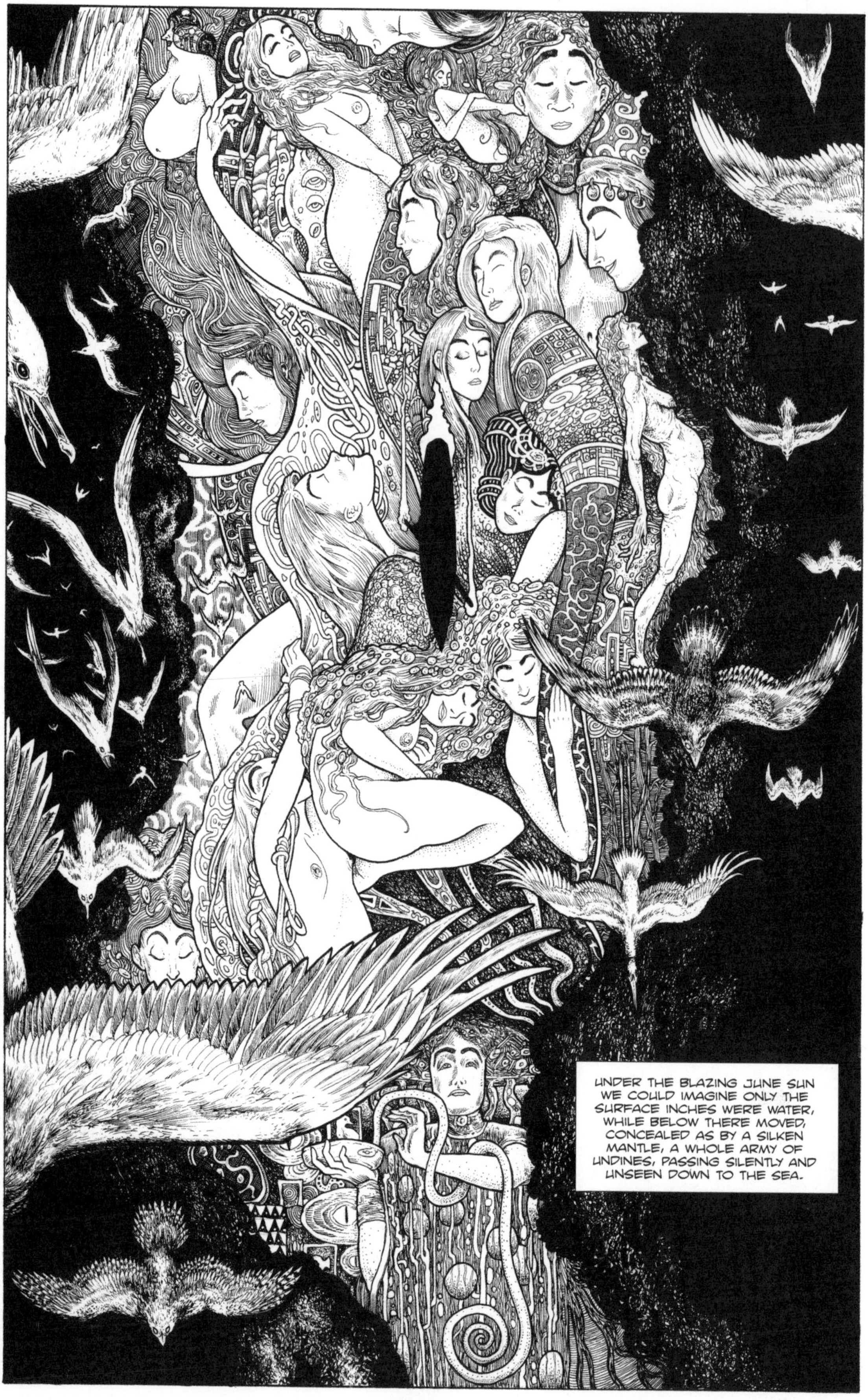
UNDER THE BLAZING JUNE SUN WE COULD IMAGINE ONLY THE SURFACE INCHES WERE WATER, WHILE BELOW THERE MOVED, CONCEALED AS BY A SILKEN MANTLE, A WHOLE ARMY OF UNDINES, PASSING SILENTLY AND UNSEEN DOWN TO THE SEA.

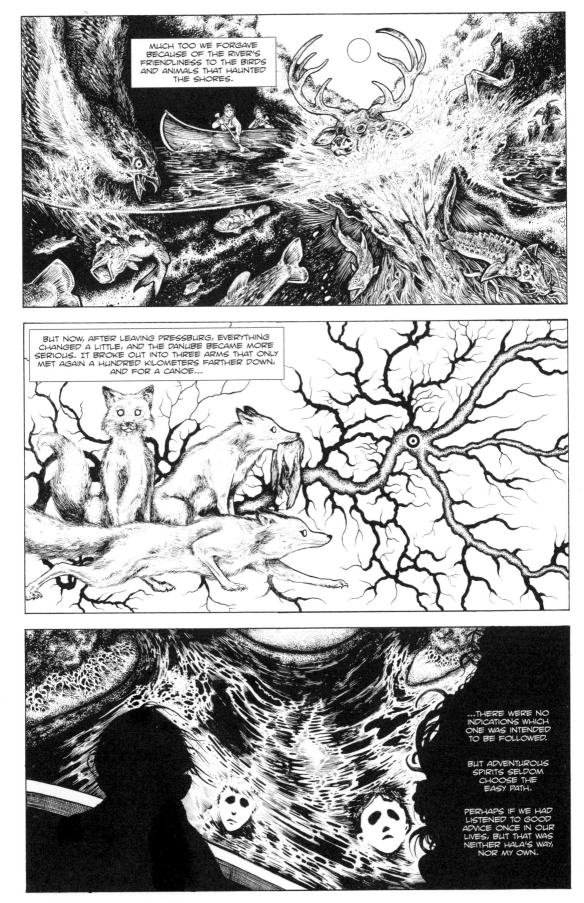

MUCH TOO WE FORGAVE BECAUSE OF THE RIVER'S FRIENDLINESS TO THE BIRDS AND ANIMALS THAT HAUNTED THE SHORES.

BUT NOW, AFTER LEAVING PRESSBURG, EVERYTHING CHANGED A LITTLE, AND THE DANUBE BECAME MORE SERIOUS. IT BROKE OUT INTO THREE ARMS THAT ONLY MET AGAIN A HUNDRED KILOMETERS FARTHER DOWN, AND FOR A CANOE...

...THERE WERE NO INDICATIONS WHICH ONE WAS INTENDED TO BE FOLLOWED.

BUT ADVENTUROUS SPIRITS SELDOM CHOOSE THE EASY PATH.

PERHAPS IF WE HAD LISTENED TO GOOD ADVICE ONCE IN OUR LIVES, BUT THAT WAS NEITHER HALA'S WAY, NOR MY OWN.

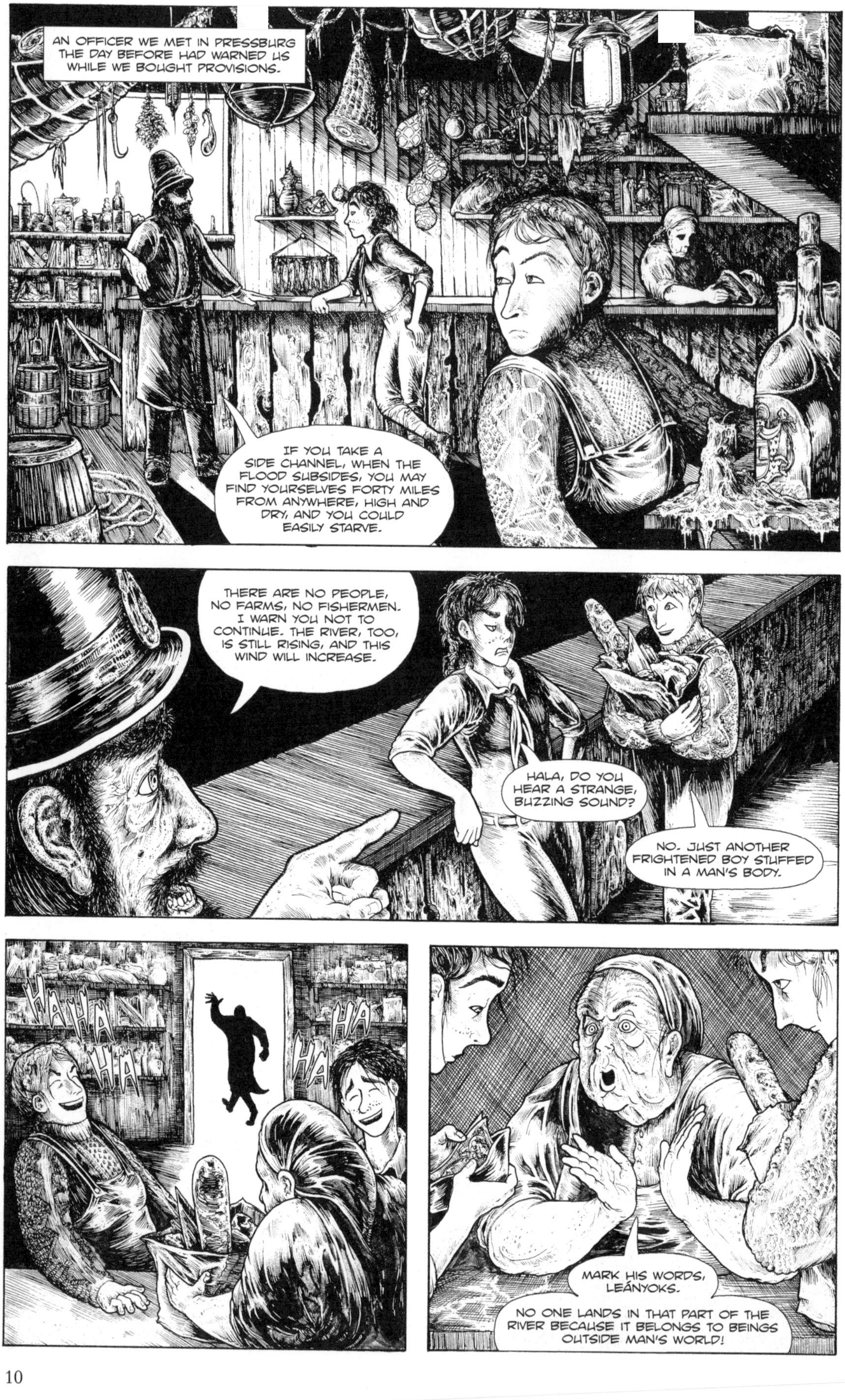

AN OFFICER WE MET IN PRESSBURG THE DAY BEFORE HAD WARNED US WHILE WE BOUGHT PROVISIONS.
IF YOU TAKE A SIDE CHANNEL, WHEN THE FLOOD SUBSIDES, YOU MAY FIND YOURSELVES FORTY MILES FROM ANYWHERE, HIGH AND DRY, AND YOU COULD EASILY STARVE.
THERE ARE NO PEOPLE, NO FARMS, NO FISHERMEN. I WARN YOU NOT TO CONTINUE. THE RIVER, TOO, IS STILL RISING, AND THIS WIND WILL INCREASE.
HALA, DO YOU HEAR A STRANGE, BUZZING SOUND?
NO. JUST ANOTHER FRIGHTENED BOY STUFFED IN A MAN'S BODY.
HA HA HA
HA HA
MARK HIS WORDS, LEÁNYOKS.
NO ONE LANDS IN THAT PART OF THE RIVER BECAUSE IT BELONGS TO BEINGS OUTSIDE MAN'S WORLD!

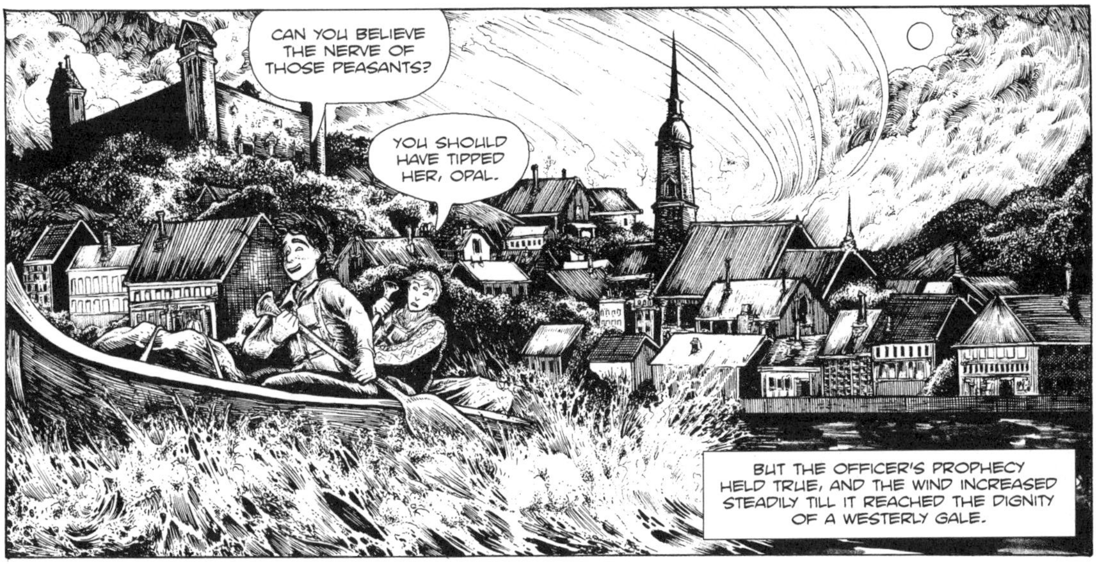
CAN YOU BELIEVE THE NERVE OF THOSE PEASANTS?
YOU SHOULD HAVE TIPPED HER, OPAL.
BUT THE OFFICER'S PROPHECY HELD TRUE, AND THE WIND INCREASED STEADILY TILL IT REACHED THE DIGNITY OF A WESTERLY GALE.

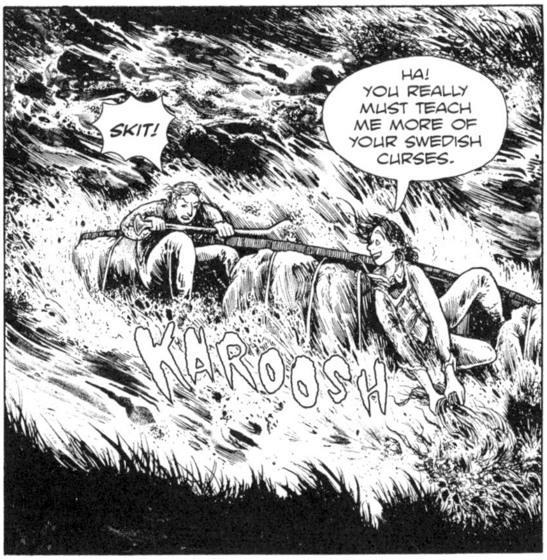
SKIT!
HA! YOU REALLY MUST TEACH ME MORE OF YOUR SWEDISH CURSES.
KAROOSH

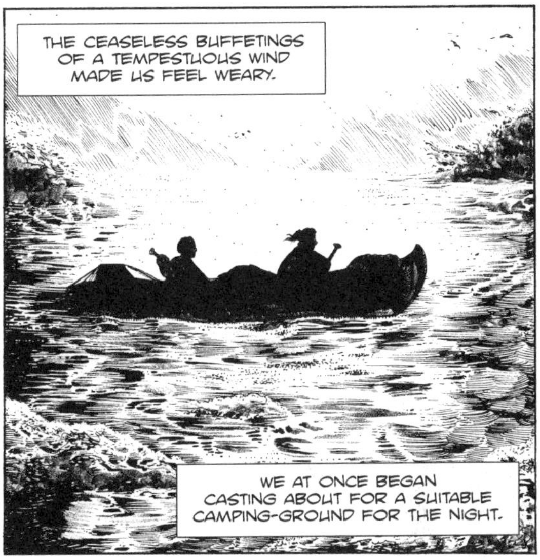
THE CEASELESS BUFFETINGS OF A TEMPESTUOUS WIND MADE US FEEL WEARY.
WE AT ONCE BEGAN CASTING ABOUT FOR A SUITABLE CAMPING-GROUND FOR THE NIGHT.

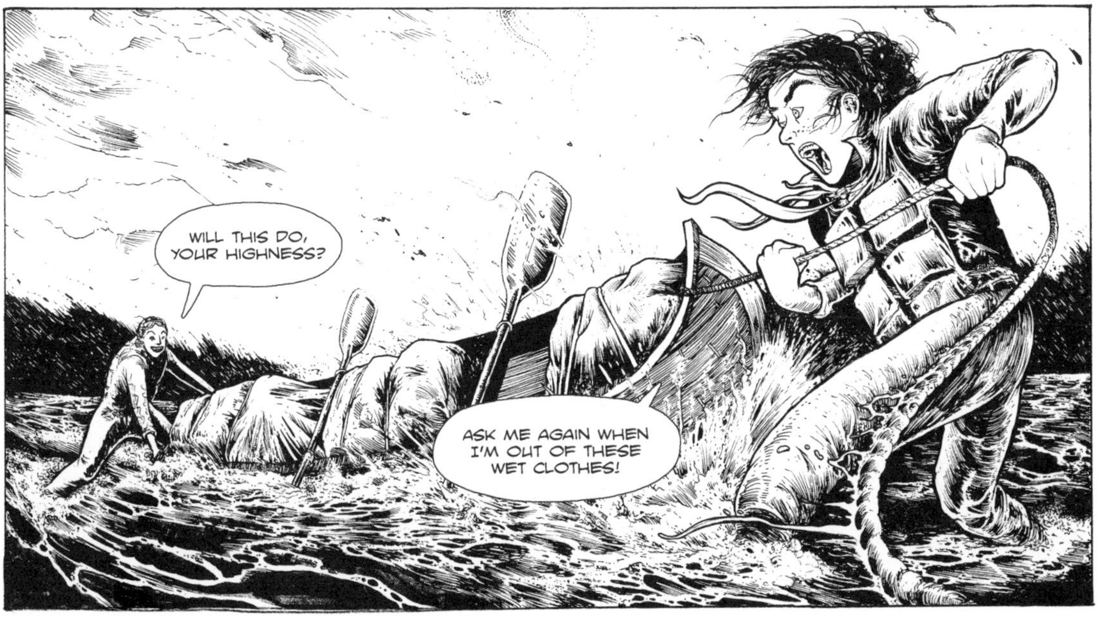
WILL THIS DO, YOUR HIGHNESS?
ASK ME AGAIN WHEN I'M OUT OF THESE WET CLOTHES!

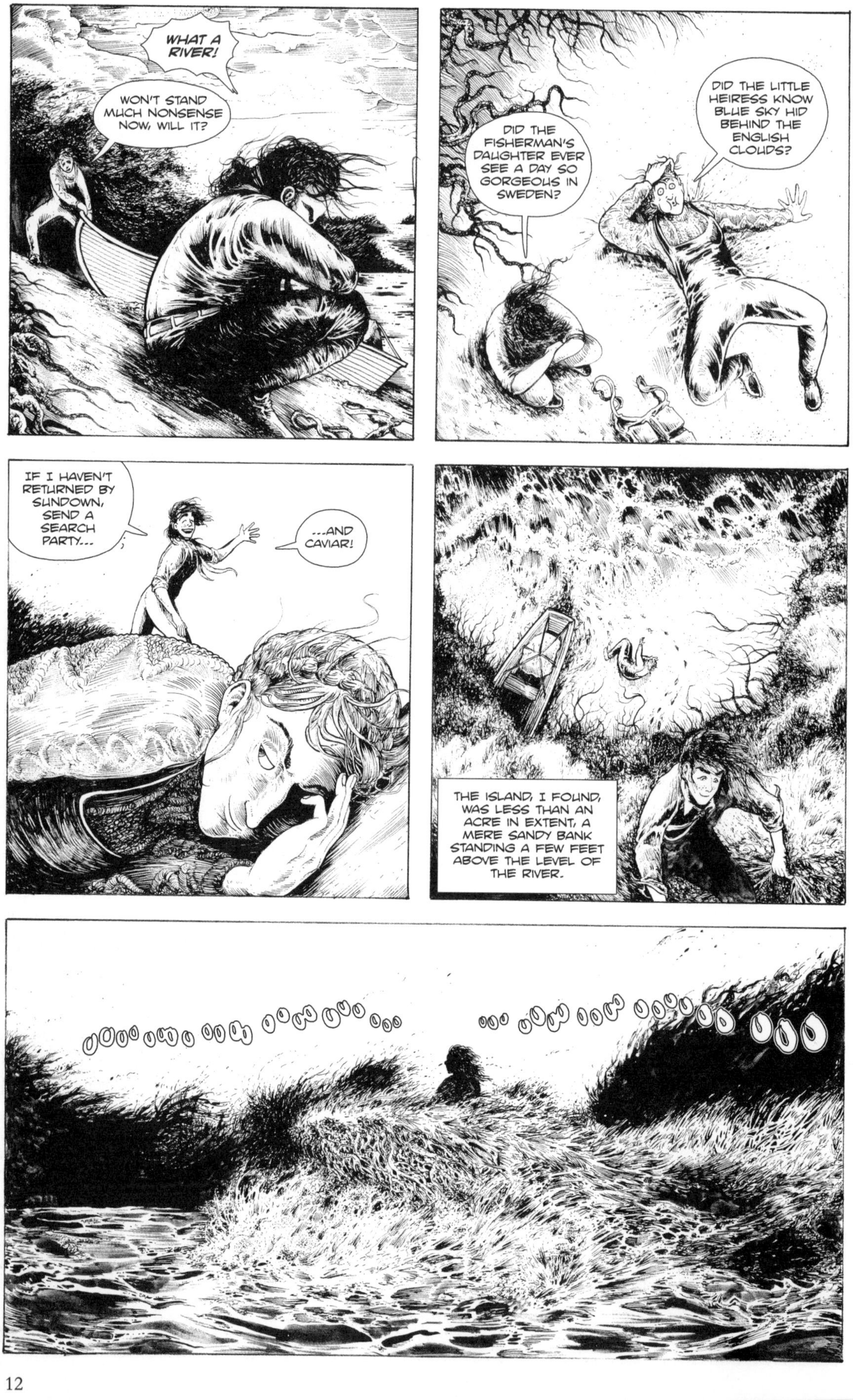
WHAT A RIVER!
WON'T STAND MUCH NONSENSE NOW, WILL IT?
DID THE FISHERMAN'S DAUGHTER EVER SEE A DAY SO GORGEOUS IN SWEDEN?
DID THE LITTLE HEIRESS KNOW BLUE SKY HID BEHIND THE ENGLISH CLOUDS?
IF I HAVEN'T RETURNED BY SUNDOWN, SEND A SEARCH PARTY...
...AND CAVIAR!
THE ISLAND, I FOUND, WAS LESS THAN AN ACRE IN EXTENT, A MERE SANDY BANK STANDING A FEW FEET ABOVE THE LEVEL OF THE RIVER.

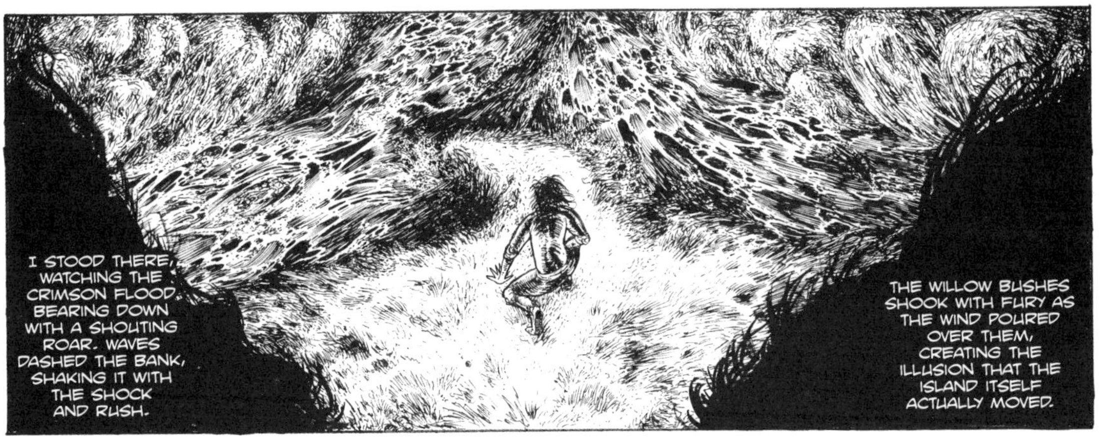
I STOOD THERE, WATCHING THE CRIMSON FLOOD BEARING DOWN WITH A SHOUTING ROAR. WAVES DASHED THE BANK, SHAKING IT WITH THE SHOCK AND RUSH.
THE WILLOW BUSHES SHOOK WITH FURY AS THE WIND POURED OVER THEM, CREATING THE ILLUSION THAT THE ISLAND ITSELF ACTUALLY MOVED.

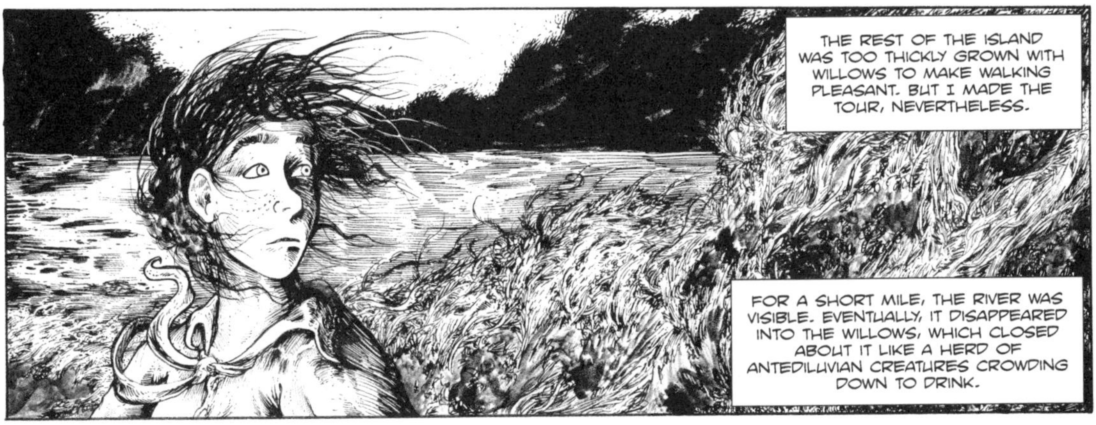
THE REST OF THE ISLAND WAS TOO THICKLY GROWN WITH WILLOWS TO MAKE WALKING PLEASANT. BUT I MADE THE TOUR, NEVERTHELESS.
FOR A SHORT MILE, THE RIVER WAS VISIBLE. EVENTUALLY, IT DISAPPEARED INTO THE WILLOWS, WHICH CLOSED ABOUT IT LIKE A HERD OF ANTEDILUVIAN CREATURES CROWDING DOWN TO DRINK.

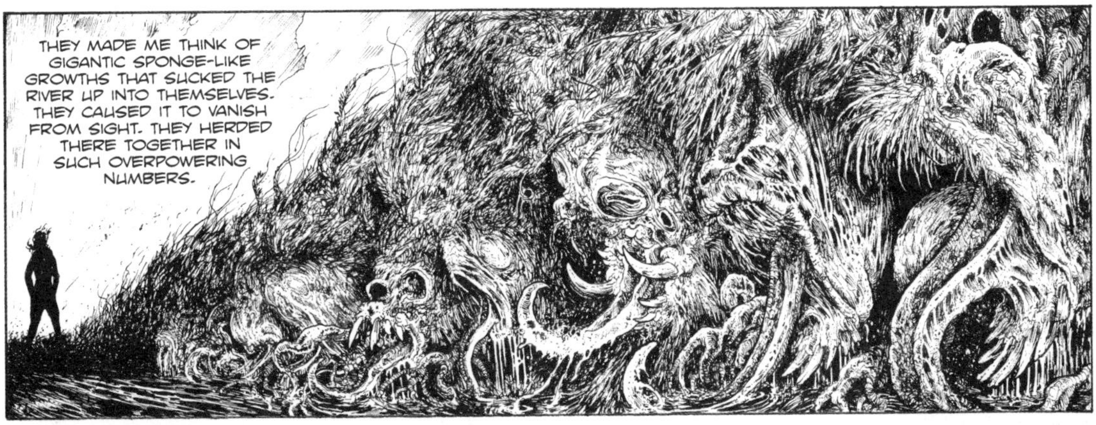
THEY MADE ME THINK OF GIGANTIC SPONGE-LIKE GROWTHS THAT SUCKED THE RIVER UP INTO THEMSELVES. THEY CAUSED IT TO VANISH FROM SIGHT. THEY HERDED THERE TOGETHER IN SUCH OVERPOWERING NUMBERS.

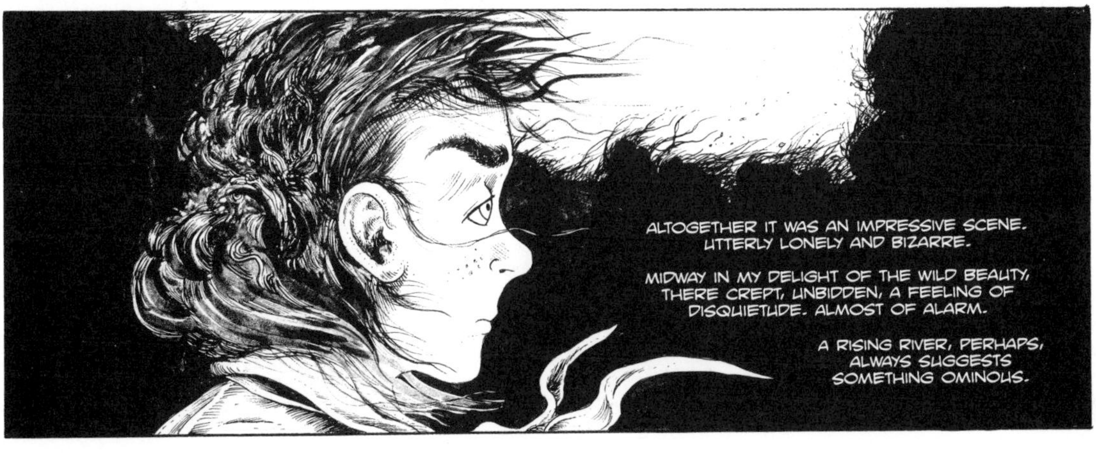
ALTOGETHER IT WAS AN IMPRESSIVE SCENE. UTTERLY LONELY AND BIZARRE.
MIDWAY IN MY DELIGHT OF THE WILD BEAUTY, THERE CREPT, UNBIDDEN, A FEELING OF DISQUIETUDE. ALMOST OF ALARM.
A RISING RIVER, PERHAPS, ALWAYS SUGGESTS SOMETHING OMINOUS.

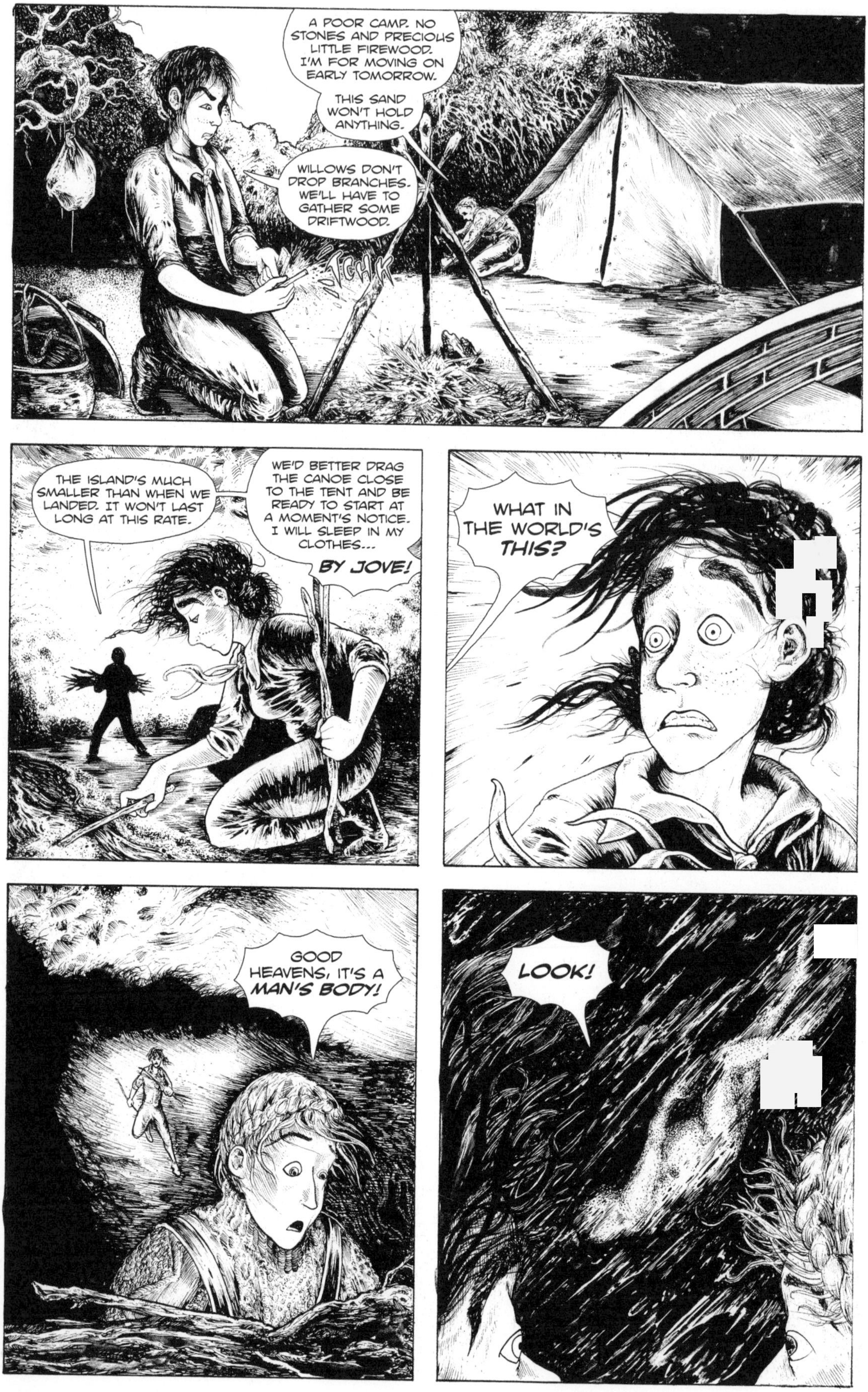
A POOR CAMP. NO STONES AND PRECIOUS LITTLE FIREWOOD. I'M FOR MOVING ON EARLY TOMORROW.
THIS SAND WON'T HOLD ANYTHING.
WILLOWS DON'T DROP BRANCHES. WE'LL HAVE TO GATHER SOME DRIFTWOOD.
TCHK
THE ISLAND'S MUCH SMALLER THAN WHEN WE LANDED. IT WON'T LAST LONG AT THIS RATE.
WE'D BETTER DRAG THE CANOE CLOSE TO THE TENT AND BE READY TO START AT A MOMENT'S NOTICE. I WILL SLEEP IN MY CLOTHES...
BY JOVE!
WHAT IN THE WORLD'S THIS?
GOOD HEAVENS, IT'S A MAN'S BODY!
LOOK!

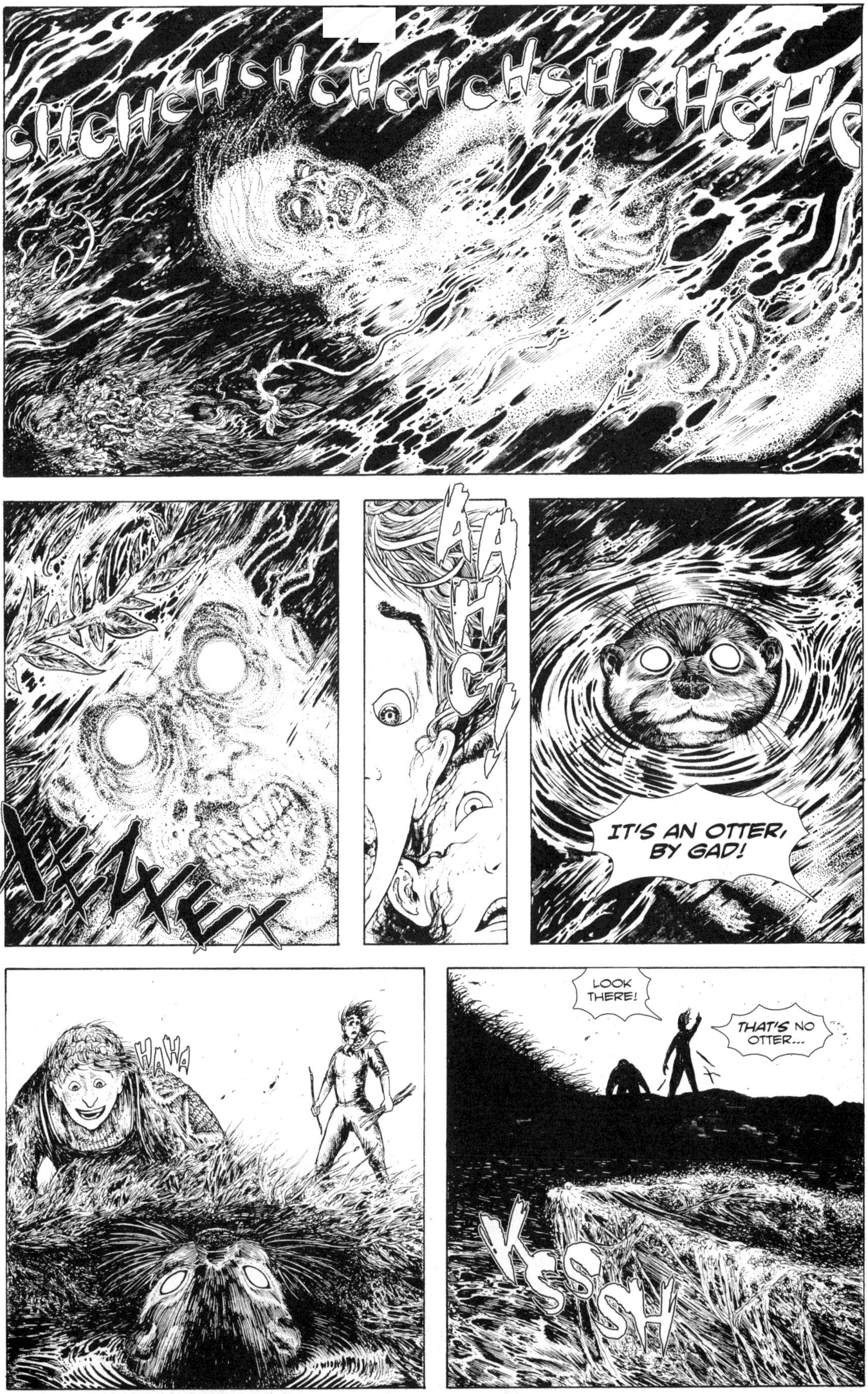
CHCHCHCHCHCHCHCHCHCHCHCHC
AAHCH!
IT'S AN OTTER, BY GAD!
HAHA
LOOK THERE!
THAT'S NO OTTER...
KSSSH

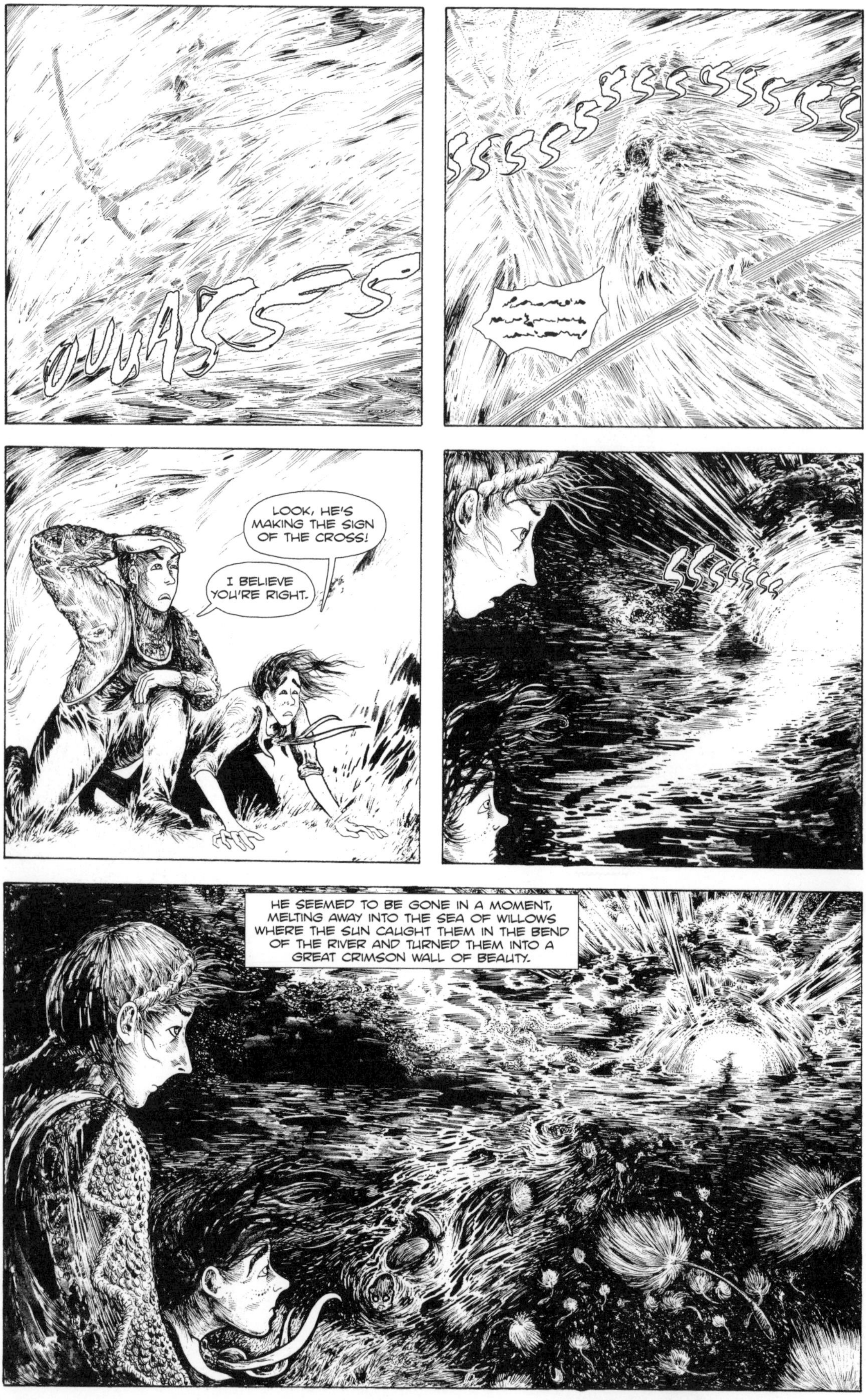
LOOK, HE'S MAKING THE SIGN OF THE CROSS!
I BELIEVE YOU'RE RIGHT.
HE SEEMED TO BE GONE IN A MOMENT, MELTING AWAY INTO THE SEA OF WILLOWS WHERE THE SUN CAUGHT THEM IN THE BEND OF THE RIVER AND TURNED THEM INTO A GREAT CRIMSON WALL OF BEAUTY.

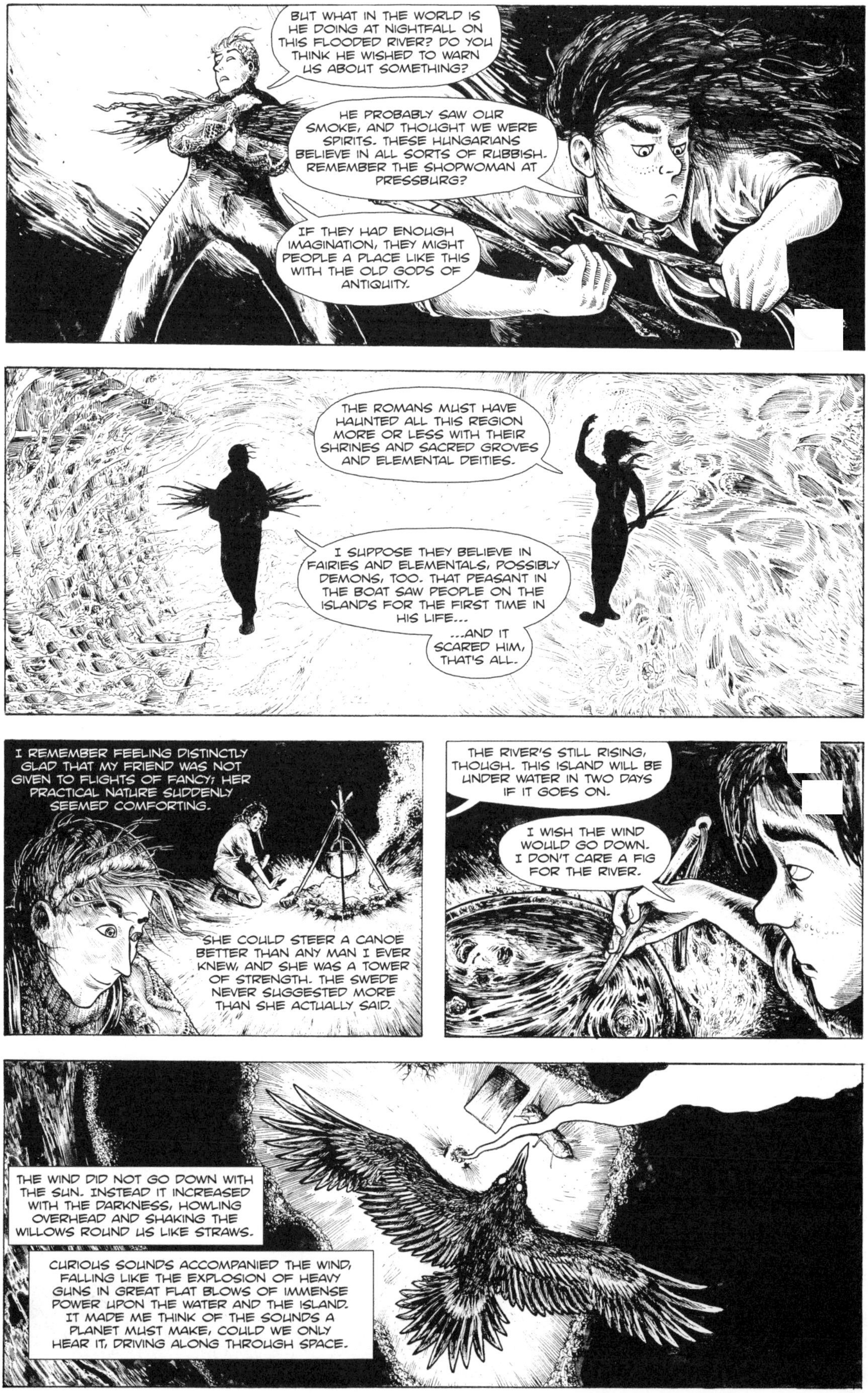
BUT WHAT IN THE WORLD IS HE DOING AT NIGHTFALL ON THIS FLOODED RIVER? DO YOU THINK HE WISHED TO WARN US ABOUT SOMETHING?
HE PROBABLY SAW OUR SMOKE, AND THOUGHT WE WERE SPIRITS. THESE HUNGARIANS BELIEVE IN ALL SORTS OF RUBBISH. REMEMBER THE SHOPWOMAN AT PRESSBURG?
IF THEY HAD ENOUGH IMAGINATION, THEY MIGHT PEOPLE A PLACE LIKE THIS WITH THE OLD GODS OF ANTIQUITY.
THE ROMANS MUST HAVE HAUNTED ALL THIS REGION MORE OR LESS WITH THEIR SHRINES AND SACRED GROVES AND ELEMENTAL DEITIES.
I SUPPOSE THEY BELIEVE IN FAIRIES AND ELEMENTALS, POSSIBLY DEMONS, TOO. THAT PEASANT IN THE BOAT SAW PEOPLE ON THE ISLANDS FOR THE FIRST TIME IN HIS LIFE...
...AND IT SCARED HIM, THAT'S ALL.
I REMEMBER FEELING DISTINCTLY GLAD THAT MY FRIEND WAS NOT GIVEN TO FLIGHTS OF FANCY; HER PRACTICAL NATURE SUDDENLY SEEMED COMFORTING.
SHE COULD STEER A CANOE BETTER THAN ANY MAN I EVER KNEW, AND SHE WAS A TOWER OF STRENGTH. THE SWEDE NEVER SUGGESTED MORE THAN SHE ACTUALLY SAID.
THE RIVER'S STILL RISING, THOUGH. THIS ISLAND WILL BE UNDER WATER IN TWO DAYS IF IT GOES ON.
I WISH THE WIND WOULD GO DOWN. I DON'T CARE A FIG FOR THE RIVER.
THE WIND DID NOT GO DOWN WITH THE SUN. INSTEAD IT INCREASED WITH THE DARKNESS, HOWLING OVERHEAD AND SHAKING THE WILLOWS ROUND US LIKE STRAWS.
CURIOUS SOUNDS ACCOMPANIED THE WIND, FALLING LIKE THE EXPLOSION OF HEAVY GUNS IN GREAT FLAT BLOWS OF IMMENSE POWER UPON THE WATER AND THE ISLAND. IT MADE ME THINK OF THE SOUNDS A PLANET MUST MAKE, COULD WE ONLY HEAR IT, DRIVING ALONG THROUGH SPACE.

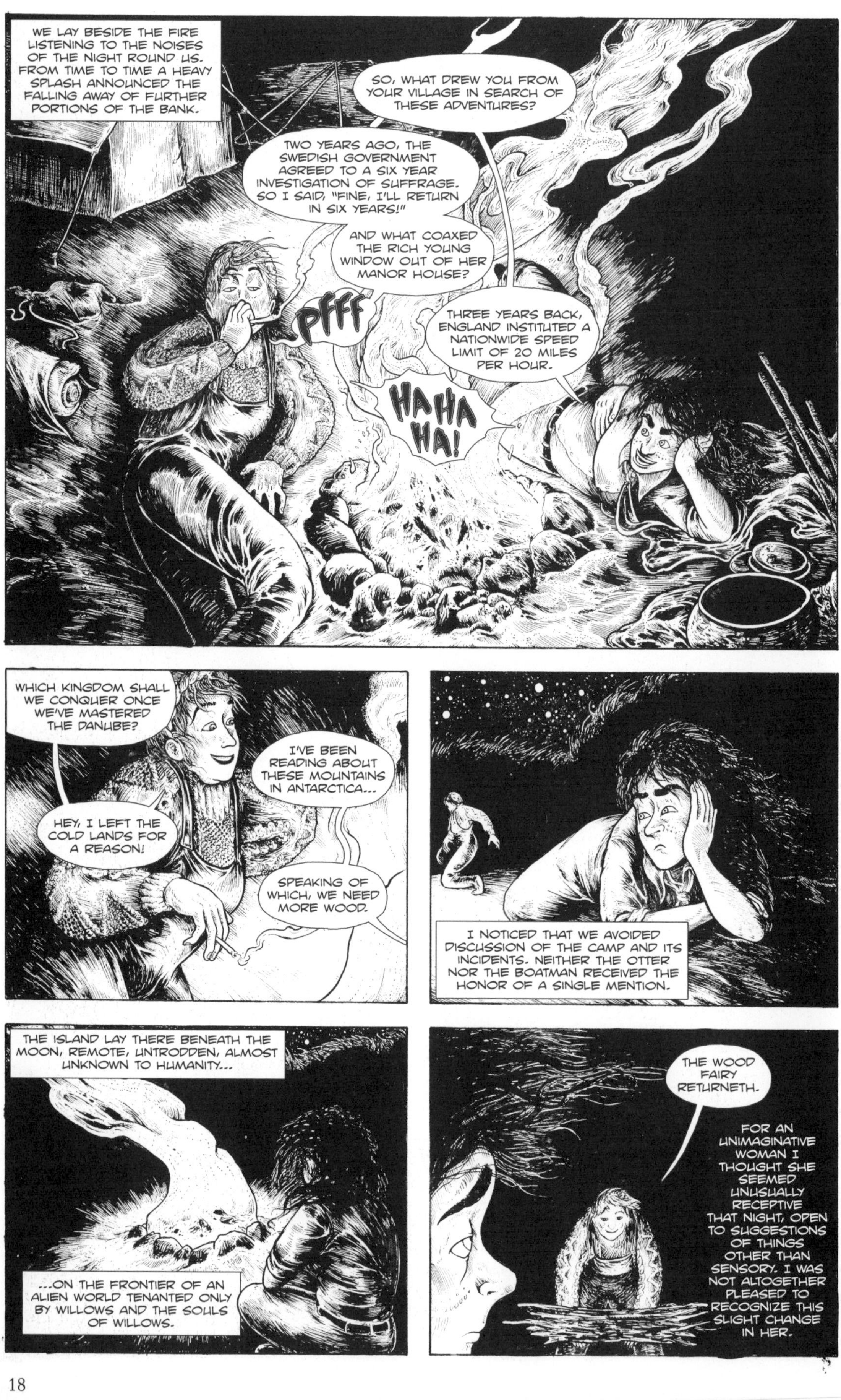
WE LAY BESIDE THE FIRE LISTENING TO THE NOISES OF THE NIGHT ROUND US. FROM TIME TO TIME A HEAVY SPLASH ANNOUNCED THE FALLING AWAY OF FURTHER PORTIONS OF THE BANK.
SO, WHAT DREW YOU FROM YOUR VILLAGE IN SEARCH OF THESE ADVENTURES?
TWO YEARS AGO, THE SWEDISH GOVERNMENT AGREED TO A SIX YEAR INVESTIGATION OF SUFFRAGE. SO I SAID, "FINE, I'LL RETURN IN SIX YEARS!"
AND WHAT COAXED THE RICH YOUNG WINDOW OUT OF HER MANOR HOUSE?
PFFF
THREE YEARS BACK, ENGLAND INSTITUTED A NATIONWIDE SPEED LIMIT OF 20 MILES PER HOUR.
HAHAHA!
WHICH KINGDOM SHALL WE CONQUER ONCE WE'VE MASTERED THE DANUBE?
I'VE BEEN READING ABOUT THESE MOUNTAINS IN ANTARCTICA...
HEY, I LEFT THE COLD LANDS FOR A REASON!
SPEAKING OF WHICH, WE NEED MORE WOOD.
I NOTICED THAT WE AVOIDED DISCUSSION OF THE CAMP AND ITS INCIDENTS. NEITHER THE OTTER NOR THE BOATMAN RECEIVED THE HONOR OF A SINGLE MENTION.
THE ISLAND LAY THERE BENEATH THE MOON, REMOTE, UNTRODDEN, ALMOST UNKNOWN TO HUMANITY...
...ON THE FRONTIER OF AN ALIEN WORLD TENANTED ONLY BY WILLOWS AND THE SOULS OF WILLOWS.
THE WOOD FAIRY RETURNETH.
FOR AN UNIMAGINATIVE WOMAN I THOUGHT SHE SEEMED UNUSUALLY RECEPTIVE THAT NIGHT, OPEN TO SUGGESTIONS OF THINGS OTHER THAN SENSORY. I WAS NOT ALTOGETHER PLEASED TO RECOGNIZE THIS SLIGHT CHANGE IN HER.

THE DESIRE TO BE ALONE CAME UPON ME. MY FORMER DREAD RETURNED IN FORCE.

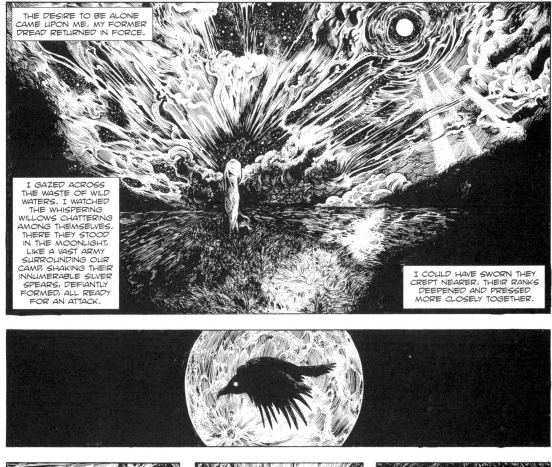

I GAZED ACROSS THE WASTE OF WILD WATERS. I WATCHED THE WHISPERING WILLOWS CHATTERING AMONG THEMSELVES. THERE THEY STOOD IN THE MOONLIGHT, LIKE A VAST ARMY SURROUNDING OUR CAMP, SHAKING THEIR INNUMERABLE SILVER SPEARS, DEFIANTLY FORMED, ALL READY FOR AN ATTACK.

I COULD HAVE SWORN THEY CREPT NEARER. THEIR RANKS DEEPENED AND PRESSED MORE CLOSELY TOGETHER.

KYEAHH!

OH!

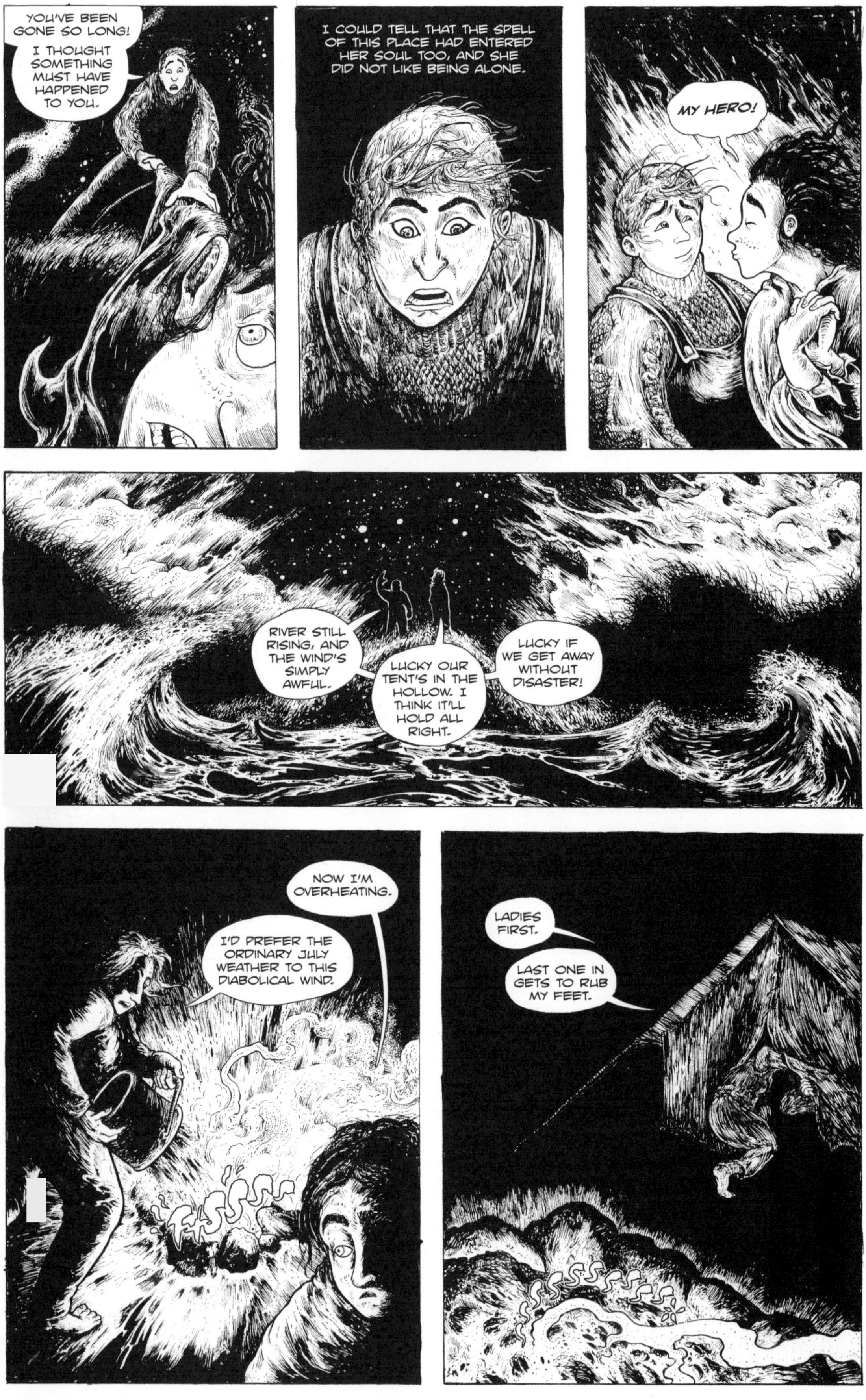
YOU'VE BEEN GONE SO LONG!
I THOUGHT SOMETHING MUST HAVE HAPPENED TO YOU.
I COULD TELL THAT THE SPELL OF THIS PLACE HAD ENTERED HER SOUL TOO, AND SHE DID NOT LIKE BEING ALONE.
MY HERO!
RIVER STILL RISING, AND THE WIND'S SIMPLY AWFUL.
LUCKY OUR TENT'S IN THE HOLLOW. I THINK IT'LL HOLD ALL RIGHT.
LUCKY IF WE GET AWAY WITHOUT DISASTER!
NOW I'M OVERHEATING.
I'D PREFER THE ORDINARY JULY WEATHER TO THIS DIABOLICAL WIND.
FSSSSS
LADIES FIRST.
LAST ONE IN GETS TO RUB MY FEET.
SSSSSS

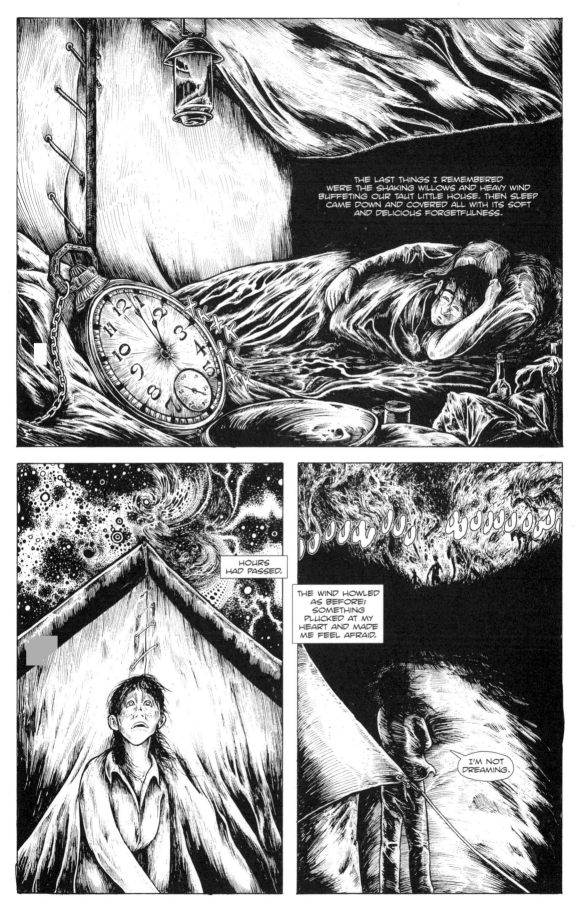

THE LAST THINGS I REMEMBERED WERE THE SHAKING WILLOWS AND HEAVY WIND BUFFETING OUR TAUT LITTLE HOUSE. THEN SLEEP CAME DOWN AND COVERED ALL WITH ITS SOFT AND DELICIOUS FORGETFULNESS.

HOURS HAD PASSED.

THE WIND HOWLED AS BEFORE; SOMETHING PLUCKED AT MY HEART AND MADE ME FEEL AFRAID.

I'M NOT DREAMING.

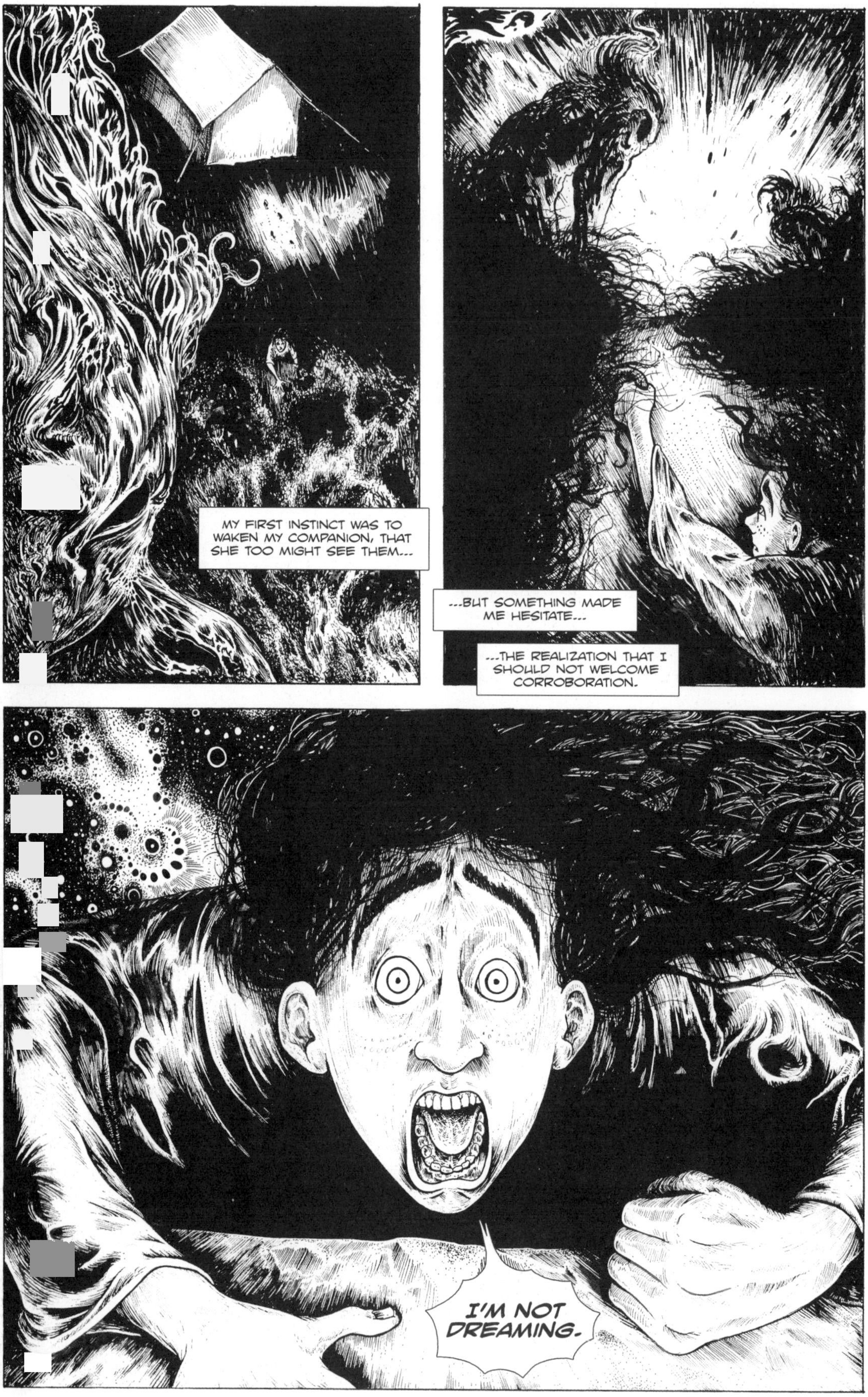
MY FIRST INSTINCT WAS TO WAKEN MY COMPANION, THAT SHE TOO MIGHT SEE THEM...
...BUT SOMETHING MADE ME HESITATE...
...THE REALIZATION THAT I SHOULD NOT WELCOME CORROBORATION.
I'M NOT DREAMING.

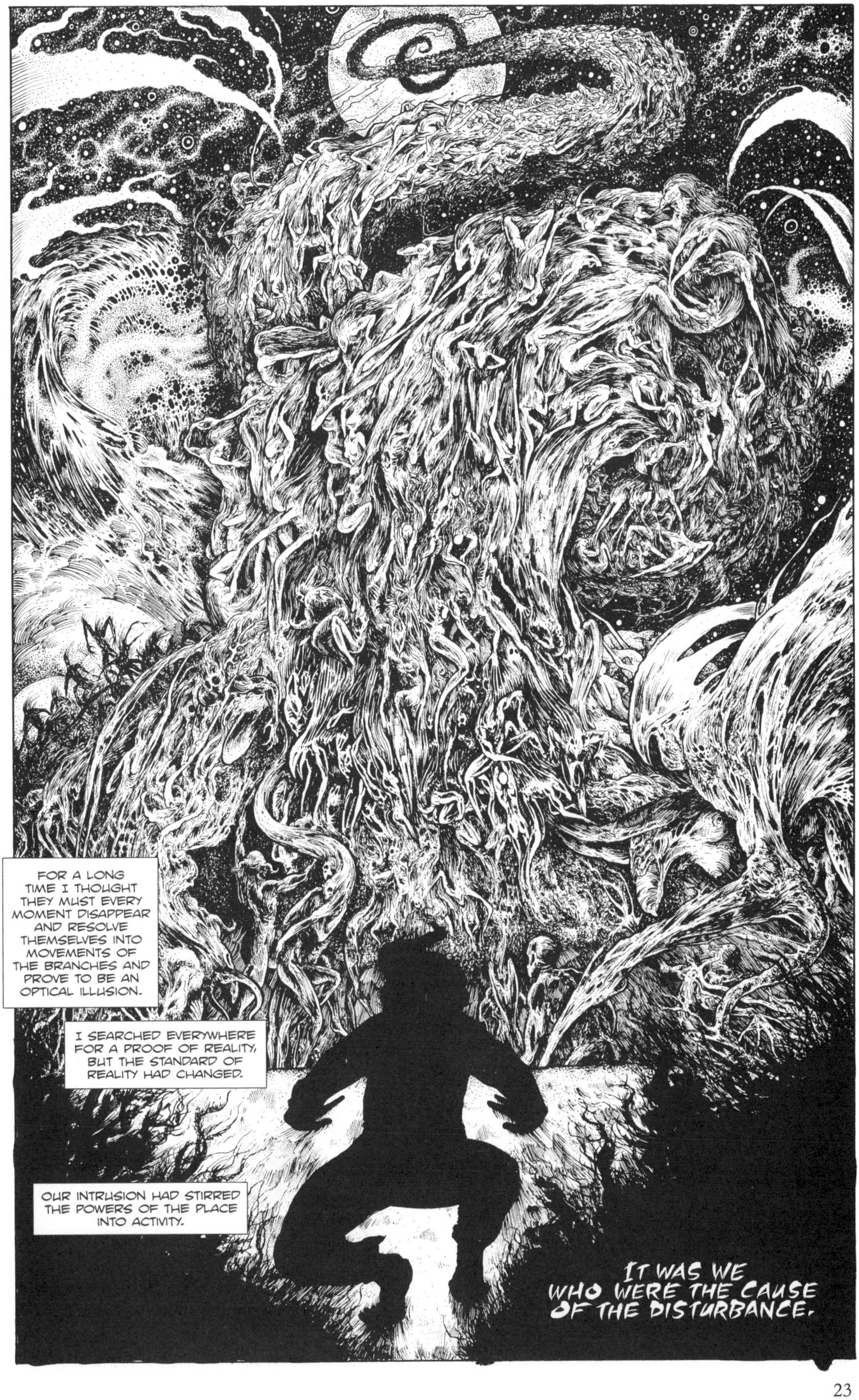
FOR A LONG TIME I THOUGHT THEY MUST EVERY MOMENT DISAPPEAR AND RESOLVE THEMSELVES INTO MOVEMENTS OF THE BRANCHES AND PROVE TO BE AN OPTICAL ILLUSION.
I SEARCHED EVERYWHERE FOR A PROOF OF REALITY, BUT THE STANDARD OF REALITY HAD CHANGED.
OUR INTRUSION HAD STIRRED THE POWERS OF THE PLACE INTO ACTIVITY.
IT WAS WE WHO WERE THE CAUSE OF THE DISTURBANCE.

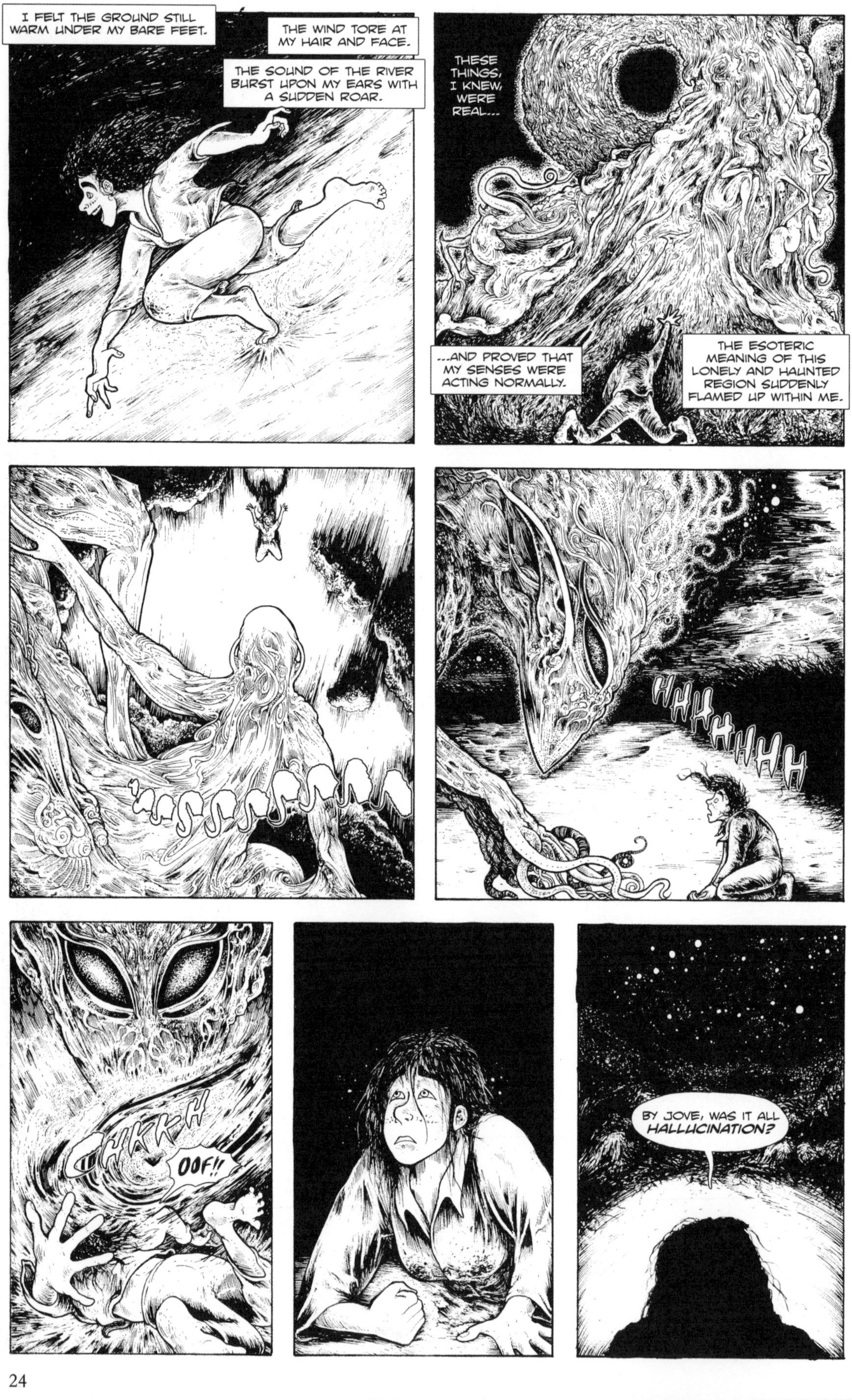

I FELT THE GROUND STILL WARM UNDER MY BARE FEET.
THE WIND TORE AT MY HAIR AND FACE.
THE SOUND OF THE RIVER BURST UPON MY EARS WITH A SUDDEN ROAR.
THESE THINGS, I KNEW, WERE REAL...
...AND PROVED THAT MY SENSES WERE ACTING NORMALLY.
THE ESOTERIC MEANING OF THIS LONELY AND HAUNTED REGION SUDDENLY FLAMED UP WITHIN ME.
CHKKKH
OOF!!
BY JOVE, WAS IT ALL HALLUCINATION?

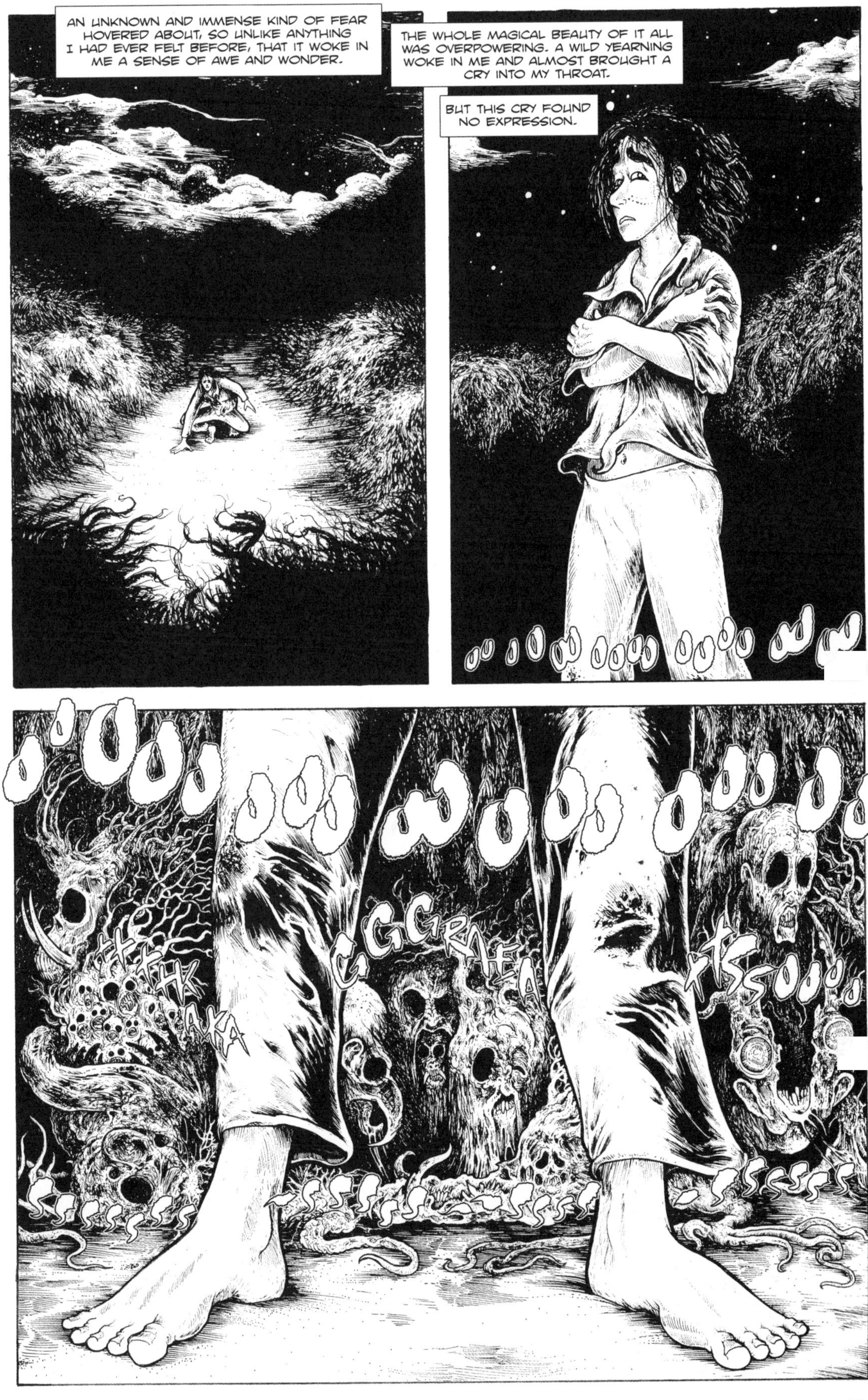
AN UNKNOWN AND IMMENSE KIND OF FEAR HOVERED ABOUT, SO UNLIKE ANYTHING I HAD EVER FELT BEFORE, THAT IT WOKE IN ME A SENSE OF AWE AND WONDER.
THE WHOLE MAGICAL BEAUTY OF IT ALL WAS OVERPOWERING. A WILD YEARNING WOKE IN ME AND ALMOST BROUGHT A CRY INTO MY THROAT.
BUT THIS CRY FOUND NO EXPRESSION.

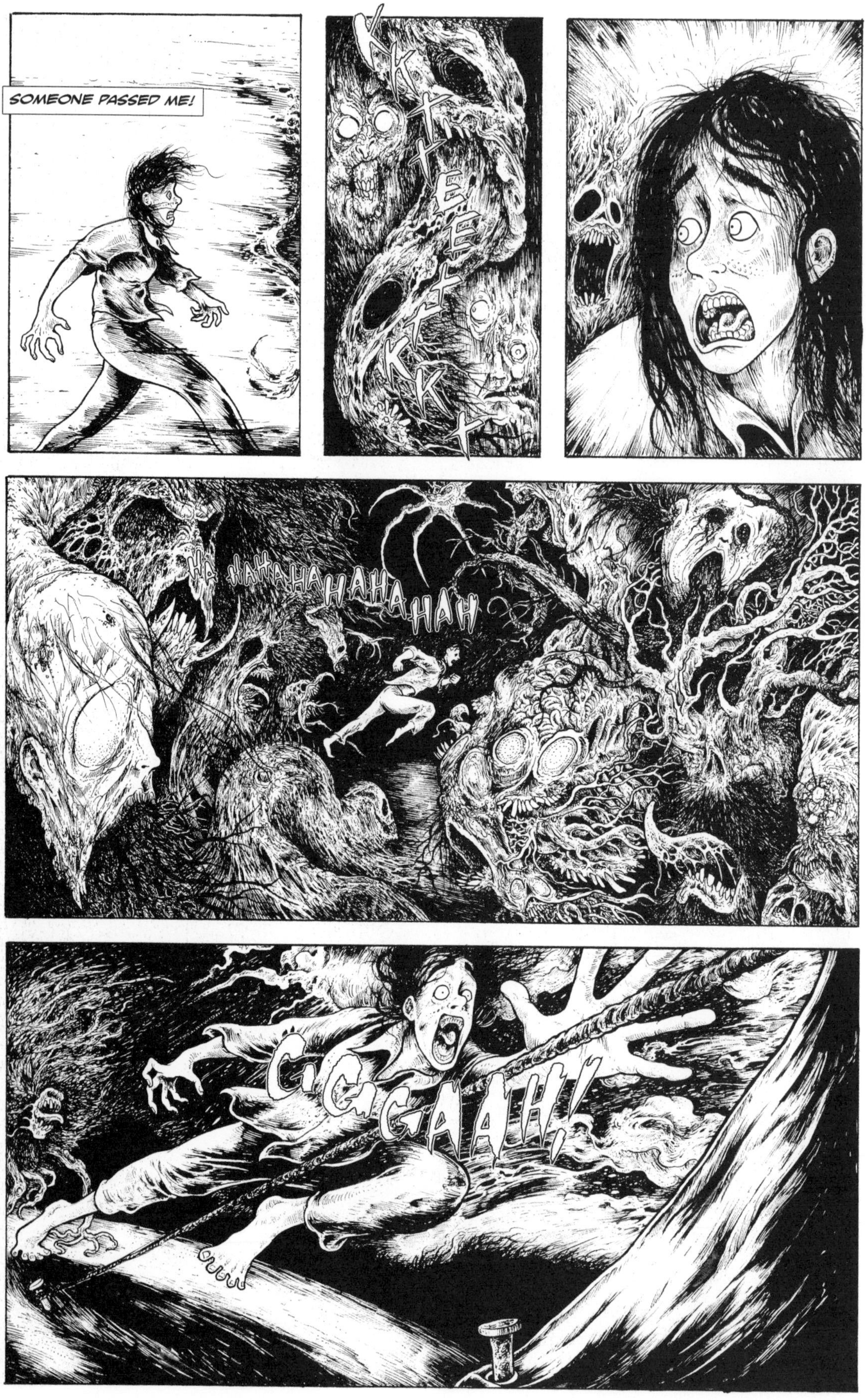
SOMEONE PASSED ME!
KKKKKHHEEEHHHKKKKHH
HA HAHAHAHAHAHAHAH
GIGGAAAH!

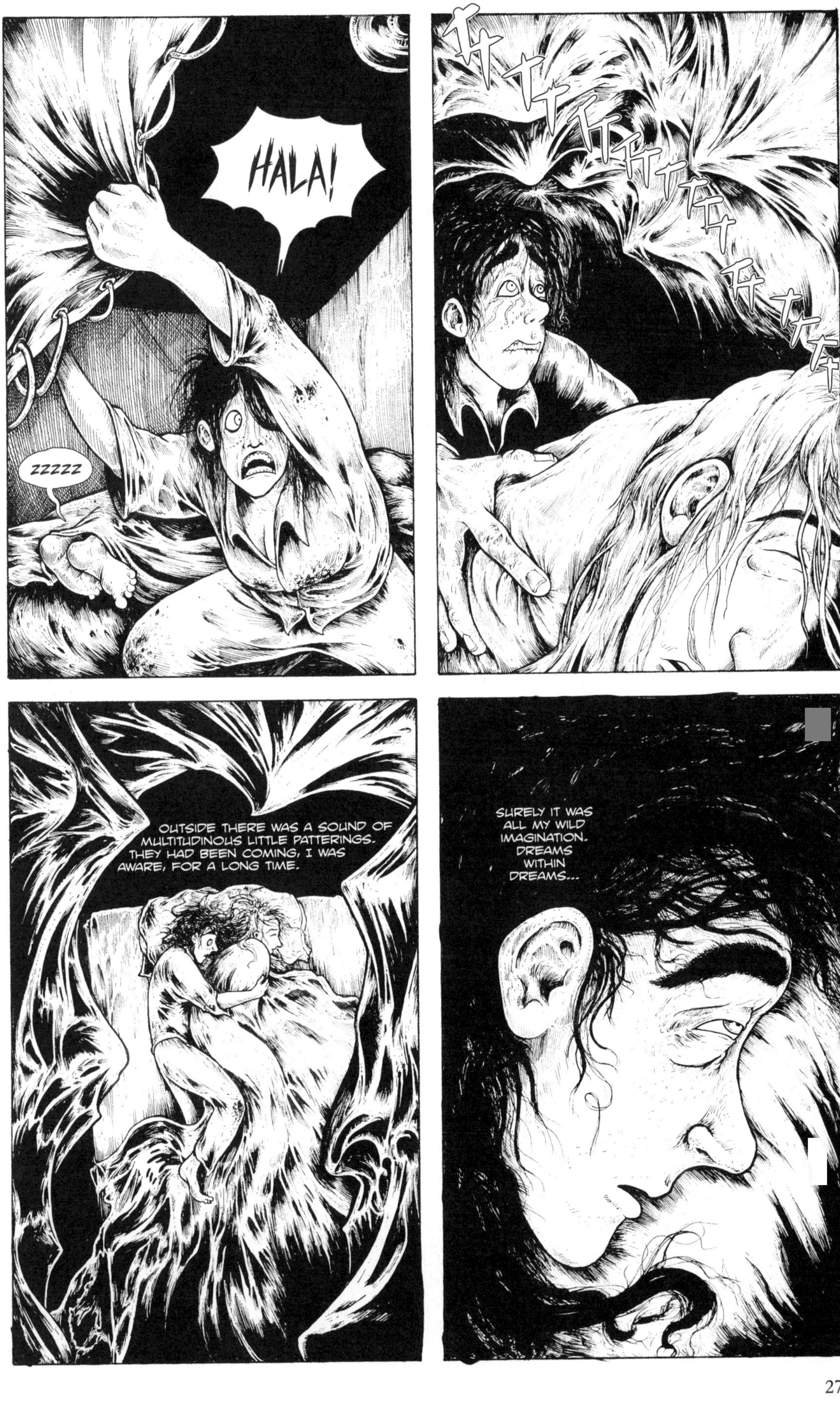
HALA!
ZZZZZ
OUTSIDE THERE WAS A SOUND OF MULTITUDINOUS LITTLE PATTERINGS. THEY HAD BEEN COMING, I WAS AWARE, FOR A LONG TIME.
SURELY IT WAS ALL MY WILD IMAGINATION. DREAMS WITHIN DREAMS...

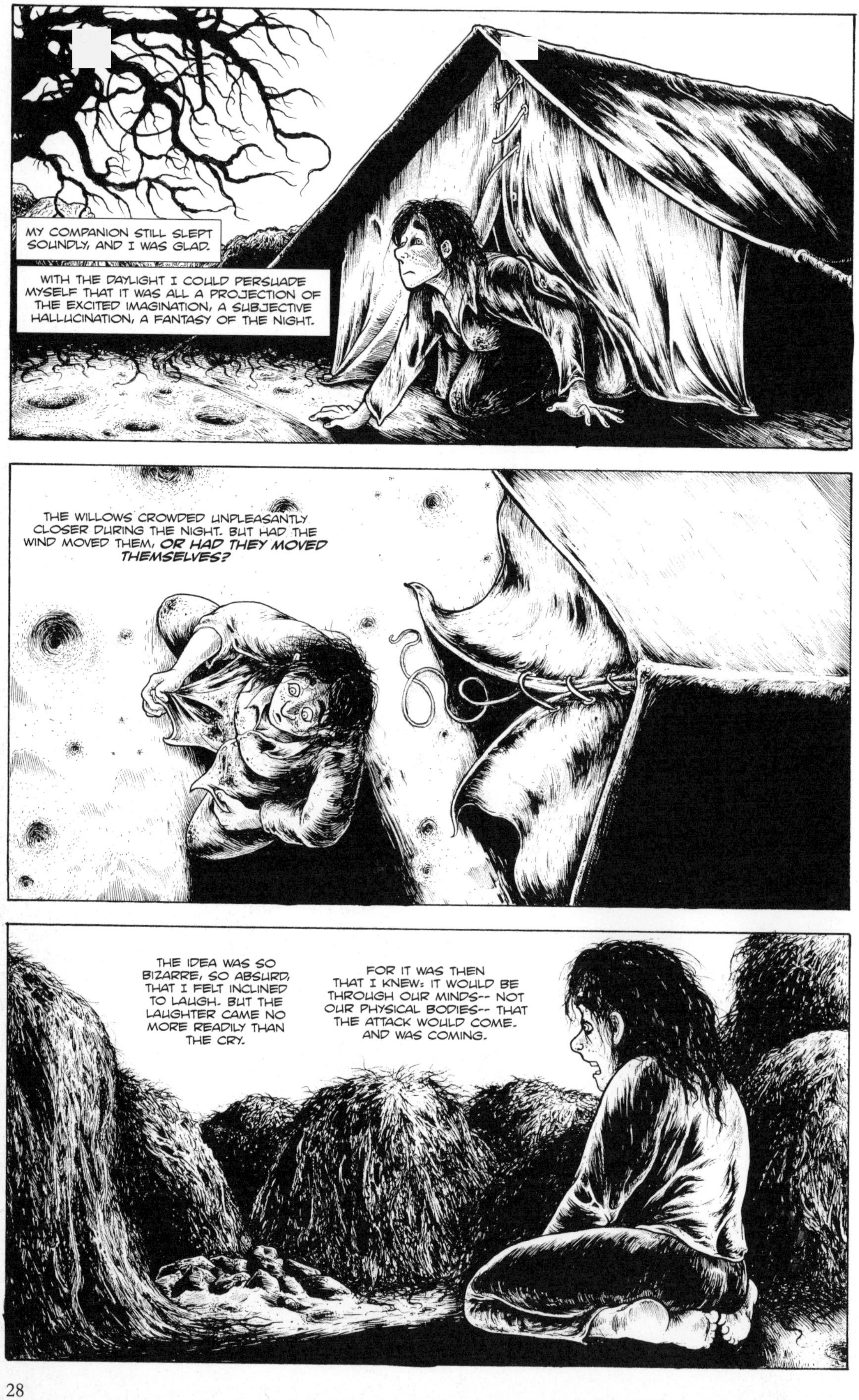
MY COMPANION STILL SLEPT SOUNDLY, AND I WAS GLAD.
WITH THE DAYLIGHT I COULD PERSUADE MYSELF THAT IT WAS ALL A PROJECTION OF THE EXCITED IMAGINATION, A SUBJECTIVE HALLUCINATION, A FANTASY OF THE NIGHT.
THE WILLOWS CROWDED UNPLEASANTLY CLOSER DURING THE NIGHT. BUT HAD THE WIND MOVED THEM, OR HAD THEY MOVED THEMSELVES?
THE IDEA WAS SO BIZARRE, SO ABSURD, THAT I FELT INCLINED TO LAUGH. BUT THE LAUGHTER CAME NO MORE READILY THAN THE CRY.
FOR IT WAS THEN THAT I KNEW: IT WOULD BE THROUGH OUR MINDS-- NOT OUR PHYSICAL BODIES-- THAT THE ATTACK WOULD COME. AND WAS COMING.

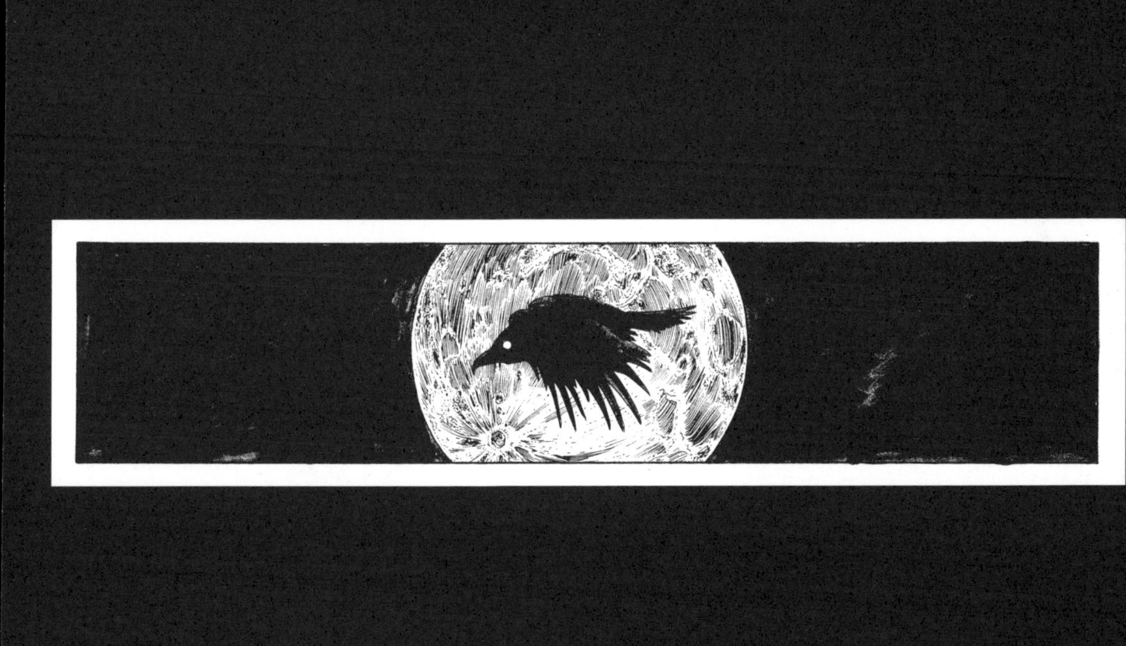

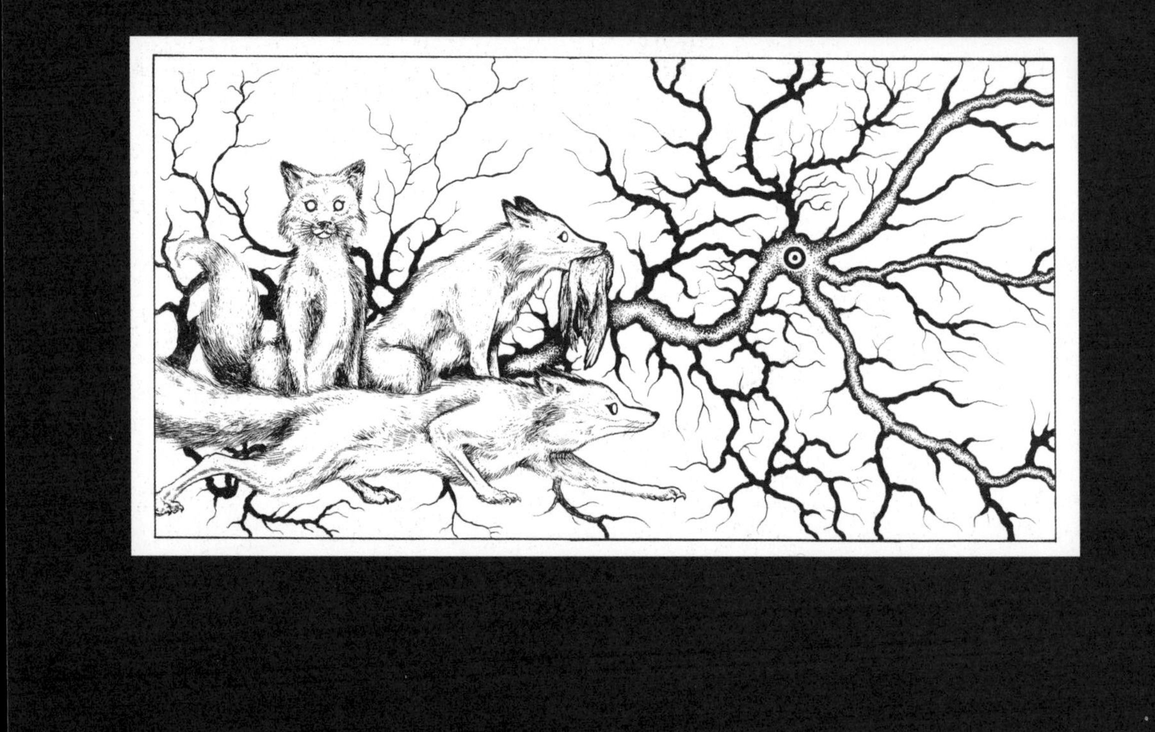

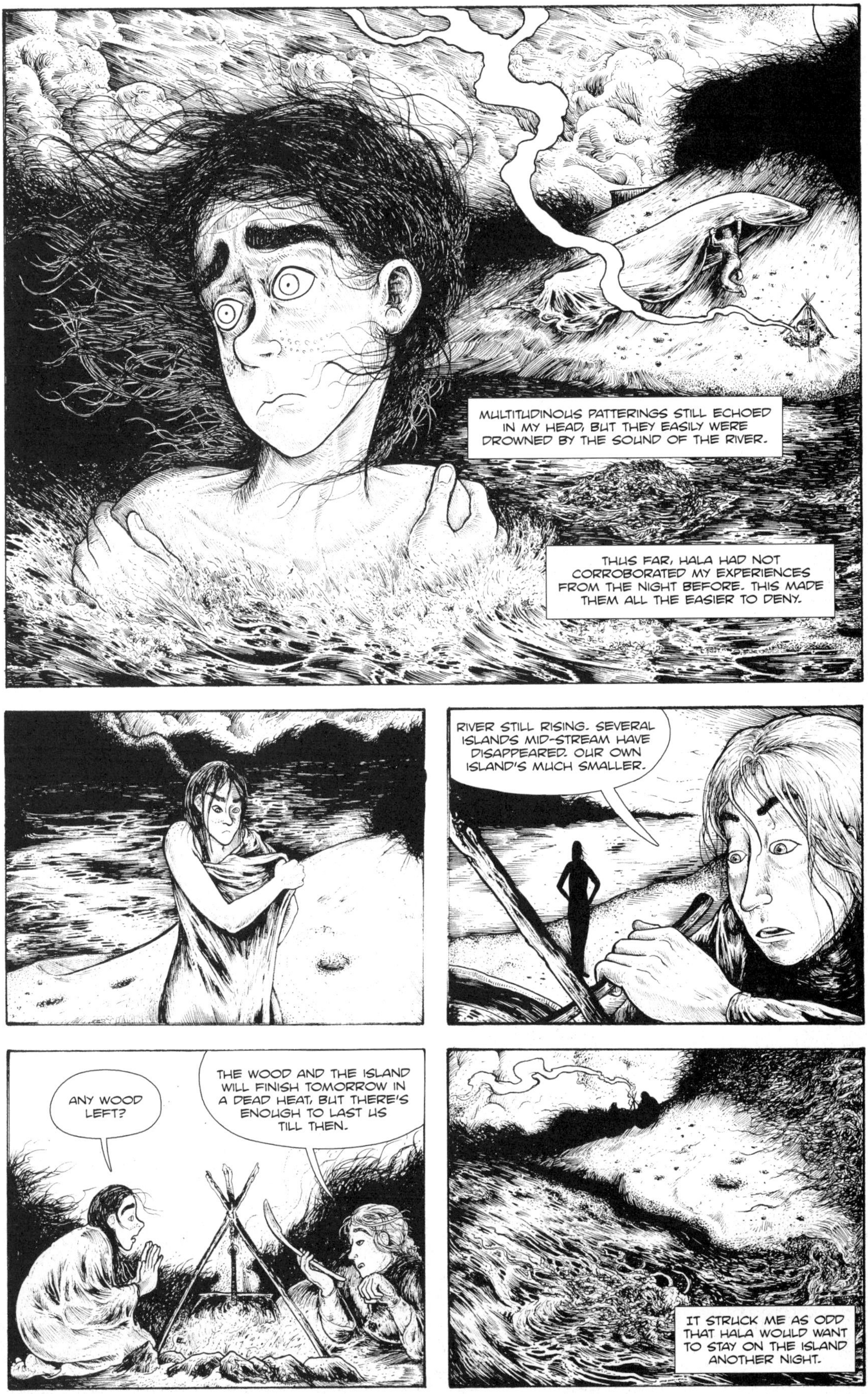
MULTITUDINOUS PATTERINGS STILL ECHOED IN MY HEAD, BUT THEY EASILY WERE DROWNED BY THE SOUND OF THE RIVER.
THUS FAR, HALA HAD NOT CORROBORATED MY EXPERIENCES FROM THE NIGHT BEFORE. THIS MADE THEM ALL THE EASIER TO DENY.
RIVER STILL RISING. SEVERAL ISLANDS MID-STREAM HAVE DISAPPEARED. OUR OWN ISLAND'S MUCH SMALLER.
ANY WOOD LEFT?
THE WOOD AND THE ISLAND WILL FINISH TOMORROW IN A DEAD HEAT, BUT THERE'S ENOUGH TO LAST US TILL THEN.
IT STRUCK ME AS ODD THAT HALA WOULD WANT TO STAY ON THE ISLAND ANOTHER NIGHT.

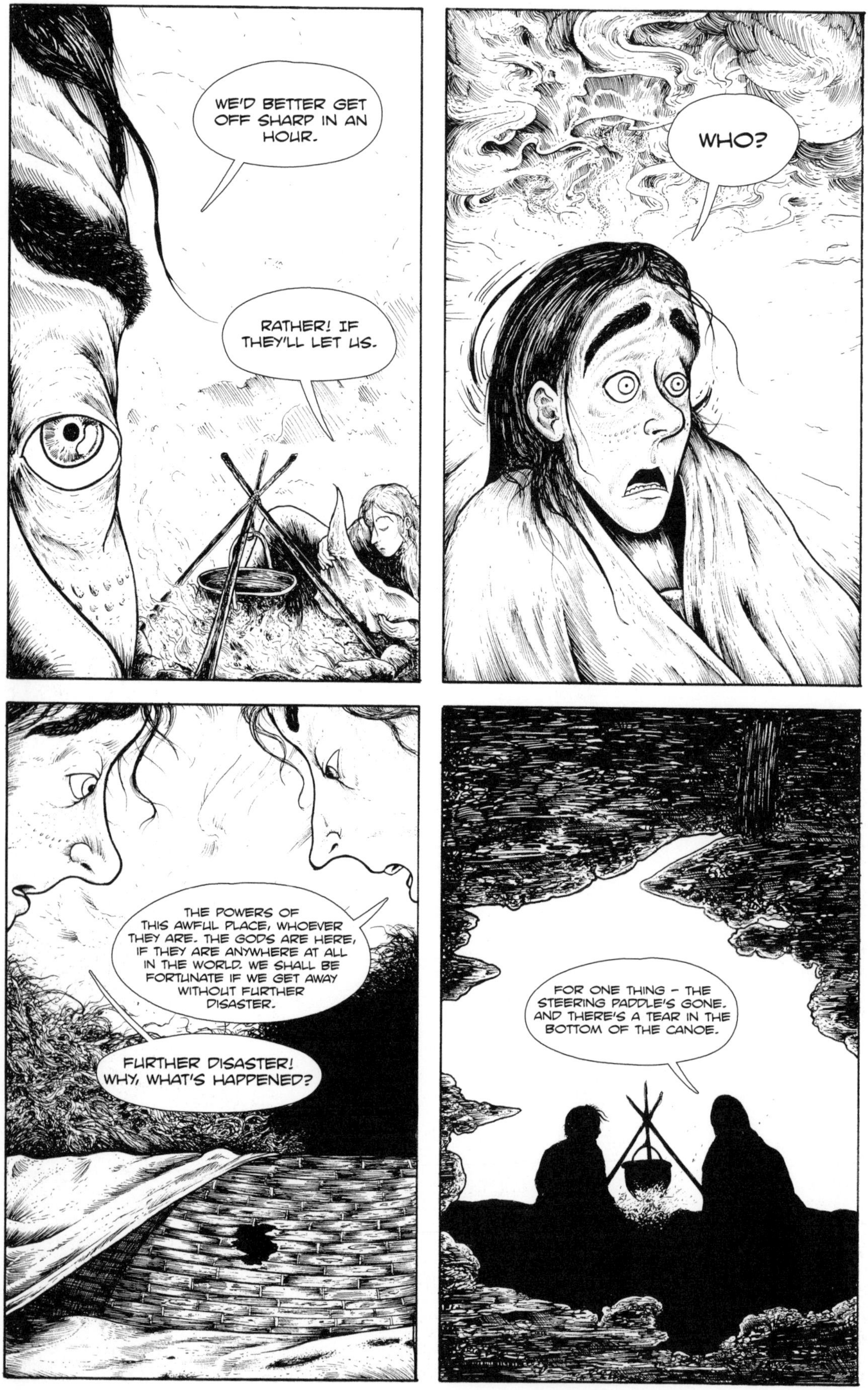

WE'D BETTER GET OFF SHARP IN AN HOUR.
RATHER! IF THEY'LL LET US.
WHO?
THE POWERS OF THIS AWFUL PLACE, WHOEVER THEY ARE. THE GODS ARE HERE, IF THEY ARE ANYWHERE AT ALL IN THE WORLD. WE SHALL BE FORTUNATE IF WE GET AWAY WITHOUT FURTHER DISASTER.
FURTHER DISASTER! WHY, WHAT'S HAPPENED?
FOR ONE THING – THE STEERING PADDLE'S GONE. AND THERE'S A TEAR IN THE BOTTOM OF THE CANOE.

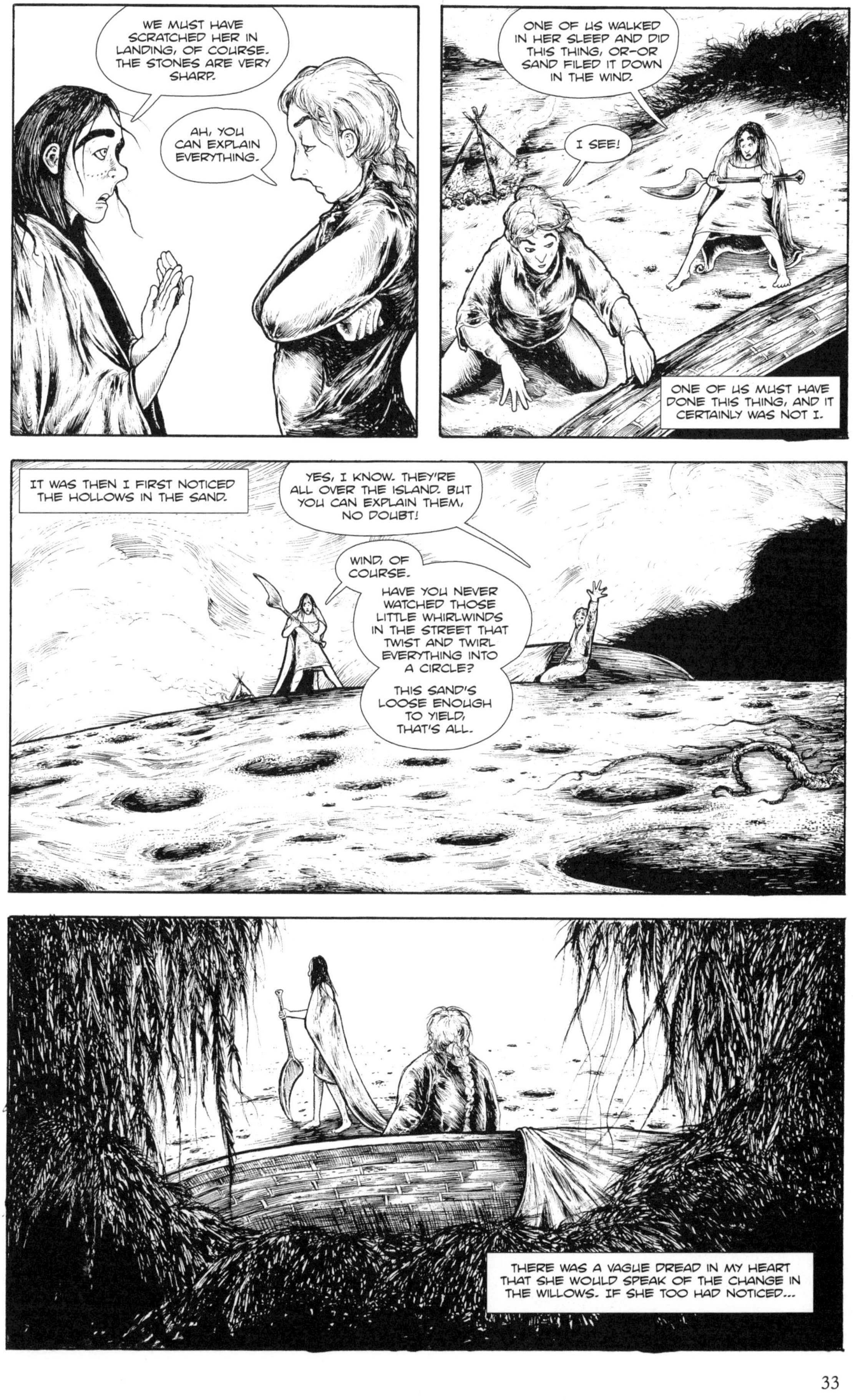
WE MUST HAVE SCRATCHED HER IN LANDING, OF COURSE. THE STONES ARE VERY SHARP.
AH, YOU CAN EXPLAIN EVERYTHING.
ONE OF US WALKED IN HER SLEEP AND DID THIS THING, OR-OR SAND FILED IT DOWN IN THE WIND.
I SEE!
ONE OF US MUST HAVE DONE THIS THING, AND IT CERTAINLY WAS NOT I.
IT WAS THEN I FIRST NOTICED THE HOLLOWS IN THE SAND.
YES, I KNOW. THEY'RE ALL OVER THE ISLAND. BUT YOU CAN EXPLAIN THEM, NO DOUBT!
WIND, OF COURSE.
HAVE YOU NEVER WATCHED THOSE LITTLE WHIRLWINDS IN THE STREET THAT TWIST AND TWIRL EVERYTHING INTO A CIRCLE?
THIS SAND'S LOOSE ENOUGH TO YIELD, THAT'S ALL.
THERE WAS A VAGUE DREAD IN MY HEART THAT SHE WOULD SPEAK OF THE CHANGE IN THE WILLOWS. IF SHE TOO HAD NOTICED...

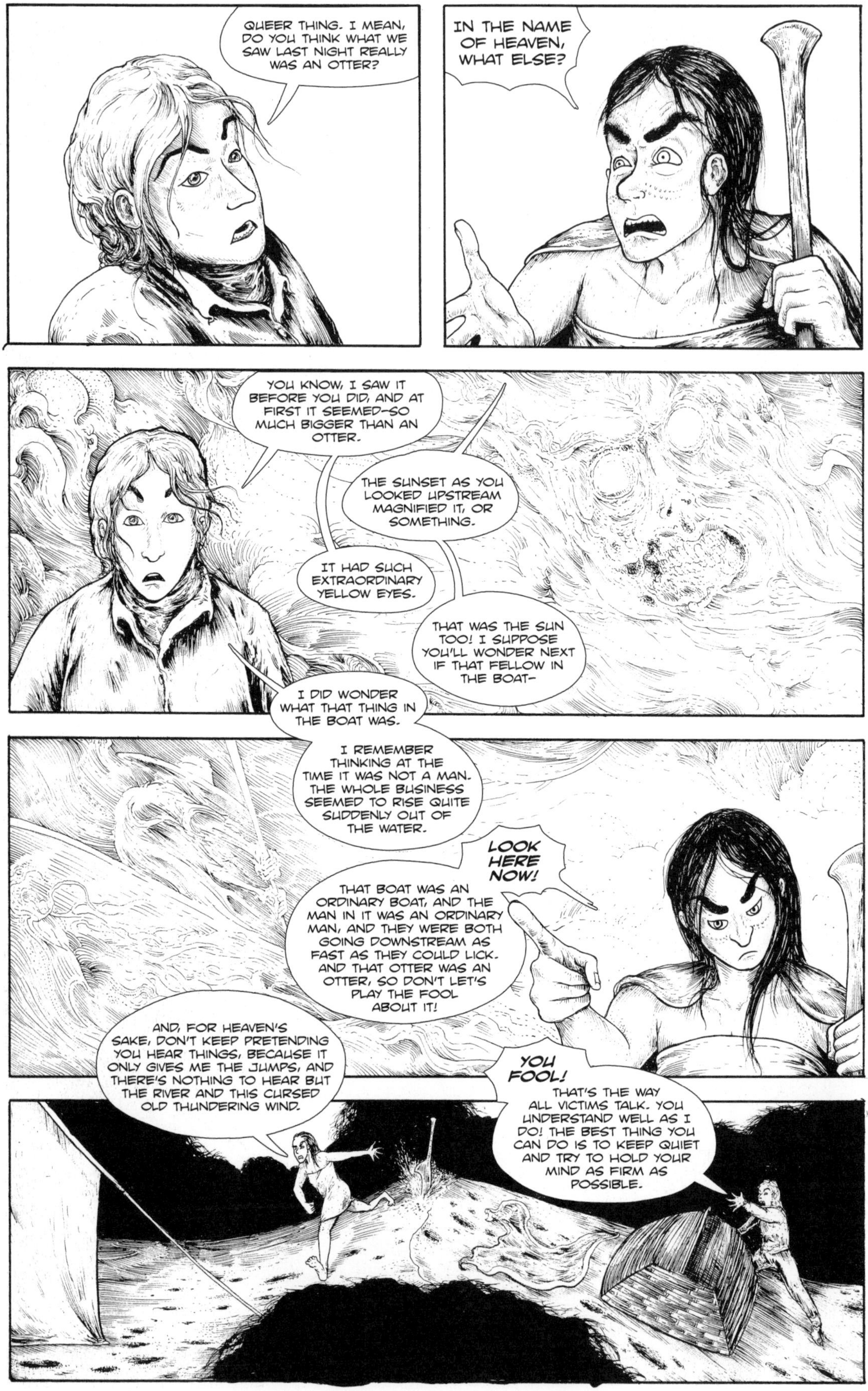
QUEER THING. I MEAN, DO YOU THINK WHAT WE SAW LAST NIGHT REALLY WAS AN OTTER?
IN THE NAME OF HEAVEN, WHAT ELSE?
YOU KNOW, I SAW IT BEFORE YOU DID, AND AT FIRST IT SEEMED–SO MUCH BIGGER THAN AN OTTER.
THE SUNSET AS YOU LOOKED UPSTREAM MAGNIFIED IT, OR SOMETHING.
IT HAD SUCH EXTRAORDINARY YELLOW EYES.
THAT WAS THE SUN TOO! I SUPPOSE YOU'LL WONDER NEXT IF THAT FELLOW IN THE BOAT–
I DID WONDER WHAT THAT THING IN THE BOAT WAS.
I REMEMBER THINKING AT THE TIME IT WAS NOT A MAN. THE WHOLE BUSINESS SEEMED TO RISE QUITE SUDDENLY OUT OF THE WATER.
LOOK HERE NOW!
THAT BOAT WAS AN ORDINARY BOAT, AND THE MAN IN IT WAS AN ORDINARY MAN, AND THEY WERE BOTH GOING DOWNSTREAM AS FAST AS THEY COULD LICK. AND THAT OTTER WAS AN OTTER, SO DON'T LET'S PLAY THE FOOL ABOUT IT!
AND, FOR HEAVEN'S SAKE, DON'T KEEP PRETENDING YOU HEAR THINGS, BECAUSE IT ONLY GIVES ME THE JUMPS, AND THERE'S NOTHING TO HEAR BUT THE RIVER AND THIS CURSED OLD THUNDERING WIND.
YOU FOOL!
THAT'S THE WAY ALL VICTIMS TALK. YOU UNDERSTAND WELL AS I DO! THE BEST THING YOU CAN DO IS TO KEEP QUIET AND TRY TO HOLD YOUR MIND AS FIRM AS POSSIBLE.

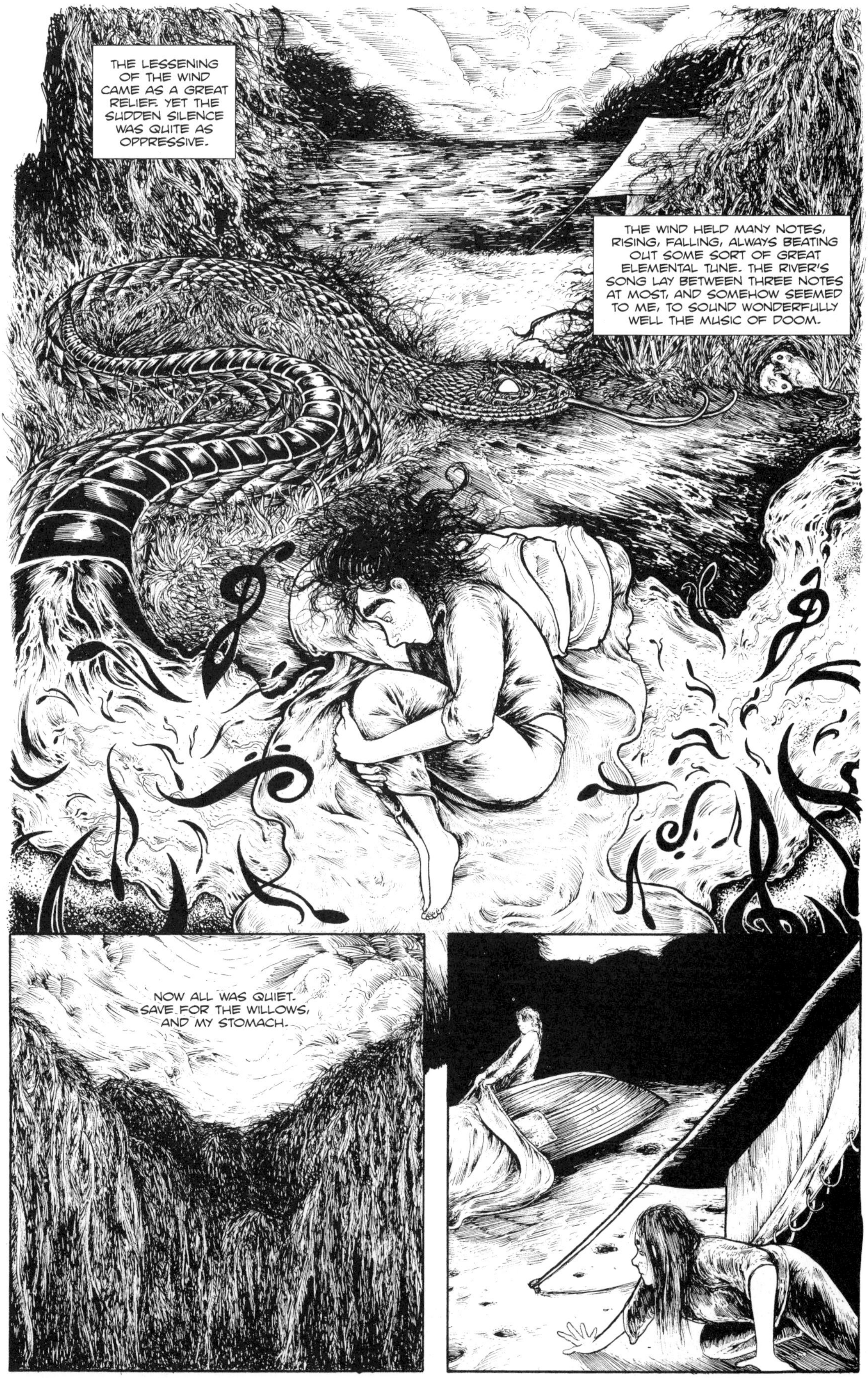
THE LESSENING OF THE WIND CAME AS A GREAT RELIEF. YET THE SUDDEN SILENCE WAS QUITE AS OPPRESSIVE.
THE WIND HELD MANY NOTES, RISING, FALLING, ALWAYS BEATING OUT SOME SORT OF GREAT ELEMENTAL TUNE. THE RIVER'S SONG LAY BETWEEN THREE NOTES AT MOST, AND SOMEHOW SEEMED TO ME, TO SOUND WONDERFULLY WELL THE MUSIC OF DOOM.
NOW ALL WAS QUIET. SAVE FOR THE WILLOWS, AND MY STOMACH.

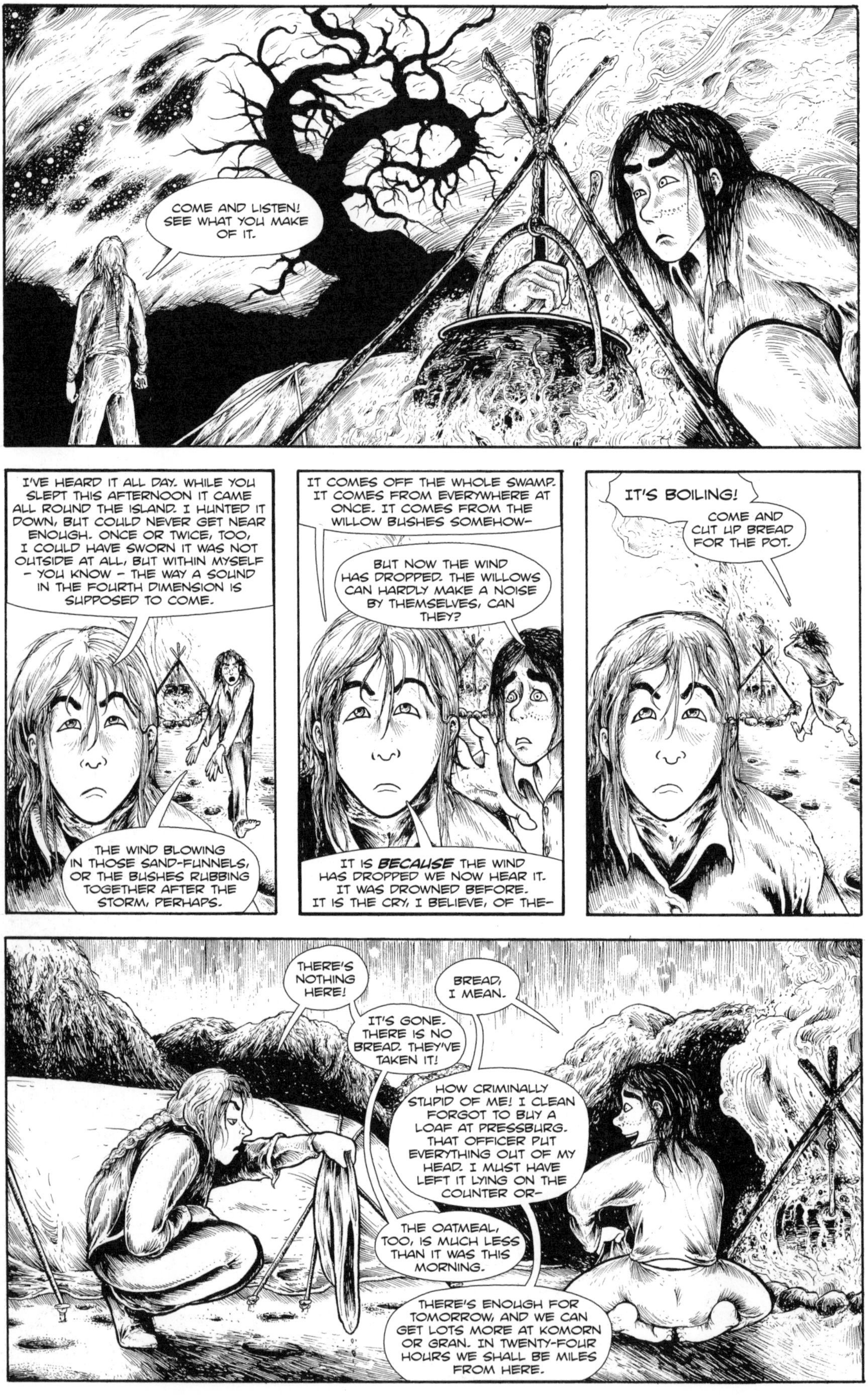
COME AND LISTEN! SEE WHAT YOU MAKE OF IT.
I'VE HEARD IT ALL DAY. WHILE YOU SLEPT THIS AFTERNOON IT CAME ALL ROUND THE ISLAND. I HUNTED IT DOWN, BUT COULD NEVER GET NEAR ENOUGH. ONCE OR TWICE, TOO, I COULD HAVE SWORN IT WAS NOT OUTSIDE AT ALL, BUT WITHIN MYSELF - YOU KNOW - THE WAY A SOUND IN THE FOURTH DIMENSION IS SUPPOSED TO COME.
THE WIND BLOWING IN THOSE SAND-FUNNELS, OR THE BUSHES RUBBING TOGETHER AFTER THE STORM, PERHAPS.
IT COMES OFF THE WHOLE SWAMP. IT COMES FROM EVERYWHERE AT ONCE. IT COMES FROM THE WILLOW BUSHES SOMEHOW-
BUT NOW THE WIND HAS DROPPED. THE WILLOWS CAN HARDLY MAKE A NOISE BY THEMSELVES, CAN THEY?
IT IS *BECAUSE* THE WIND HAS DROPPED WE NOW HEAR IT. IT WAS DROWNED BEFORE. IT IS THE CRY, I BELIEVE, OF THE-
IT'S BOILING!
COME AND CUT UP BREAD FOR THE POT.
THERE'S NOTHING HERE!
IT'S GONE. THERE IS NO BREAD. THEY'VE TAKEN IT!
BREAD, I MEAN.
HOW CRIMINALLY STUPID OF ME! I CLEAN FORGOT TO BUY A LOAF AT PRESSBURG. THAT OFFICER PUT EVERYTHING OUT OF MY HEAD. I MUST HAVE LEFT IT LYING ON THE COUNTER OR-
THE OATMEAL, TOO, IS MUCH LESS THAN IT WAS THIS MORNING.
THERE'S ENOUGH FOR TOMORROW, AND WE CAN GET LOTS MORE AT KOMORN OR GRAN. IN TWENTY-FOUR HOURS WE SHALL BE MILES FROM HERE.

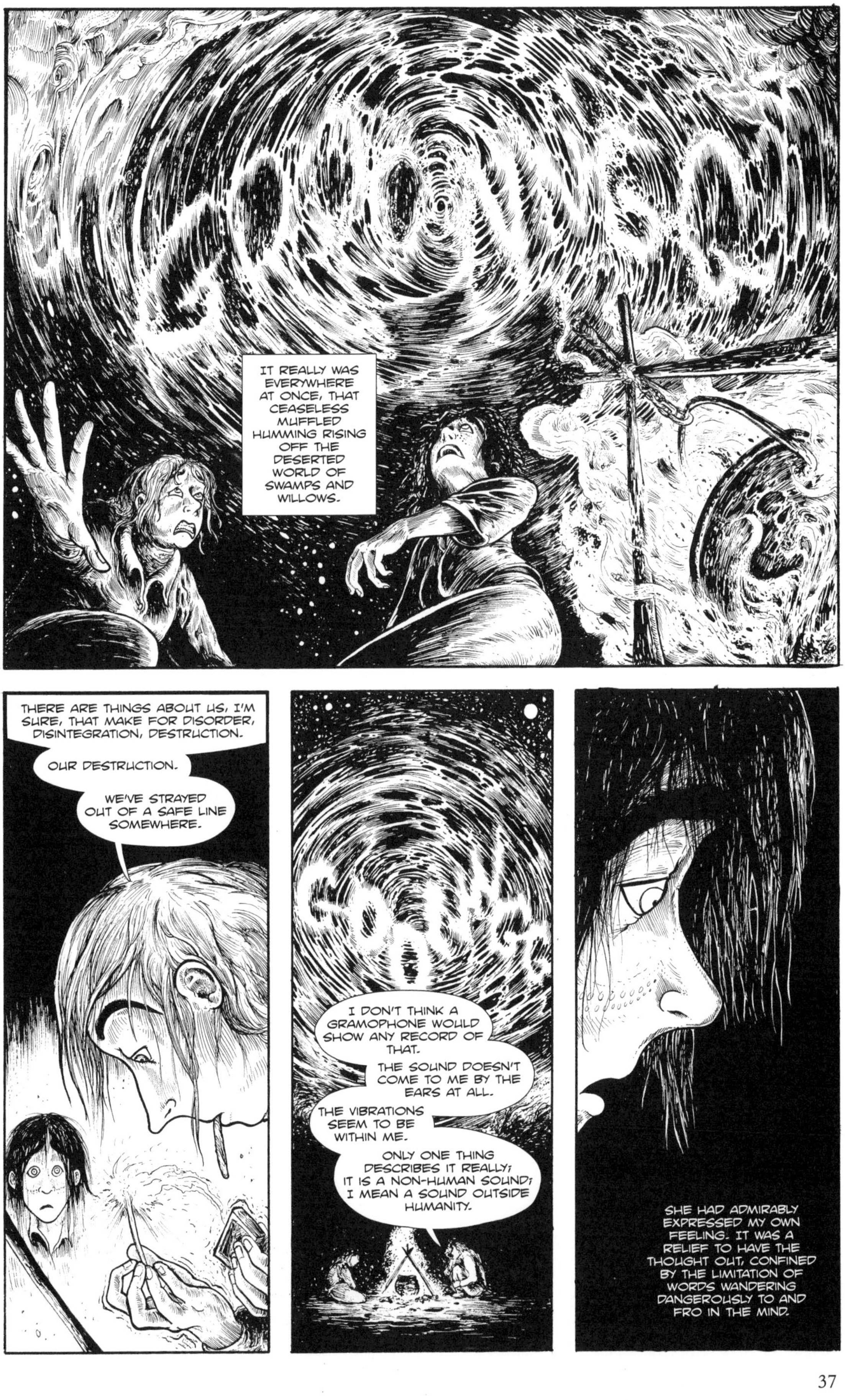
IT REALLY WAS EVERYWHERE AT ONCE, THAT CEASELESS MUFFLED HUMMING RISING OFF THE DESERTED WORLD OF SWAMPS AND WILLOWS.
THERE ARE THINGS ABOUT US, I'M SURE, THAT MAKE FOR DISORDER, DISINTEGRATION, DESTRUCTION.
OUR DESTRUCTION.
WE'VE STRAYED OUT OF A SAFE LINE SOMEWHERE.
I DON'T THINK A GRAMOPHONE WOULD SHOW ANY RECORD OF THAT.
THE SOUND DOESN'T COME TO ME BY THE EARS AT ALL.
THE VIBRATIONS SEEM TO BE WITHIN ME.
ONLY ONE THING DESCRIBES IT REALLY; IT IS A NON-HUMAN SOUND; I MEAN A SOUND OUTSIDE HUMANITY.
SHE HAD ADMIRABLY EXPRESSED MY OWN FEELING. IT WAS A RELIEF TO HAVE THE THOUGHT OUT, CONFINED BY THE LIMITATION OF WORDS WANDERING DANGEROUSLY TO AND FRO IN THE MIND.

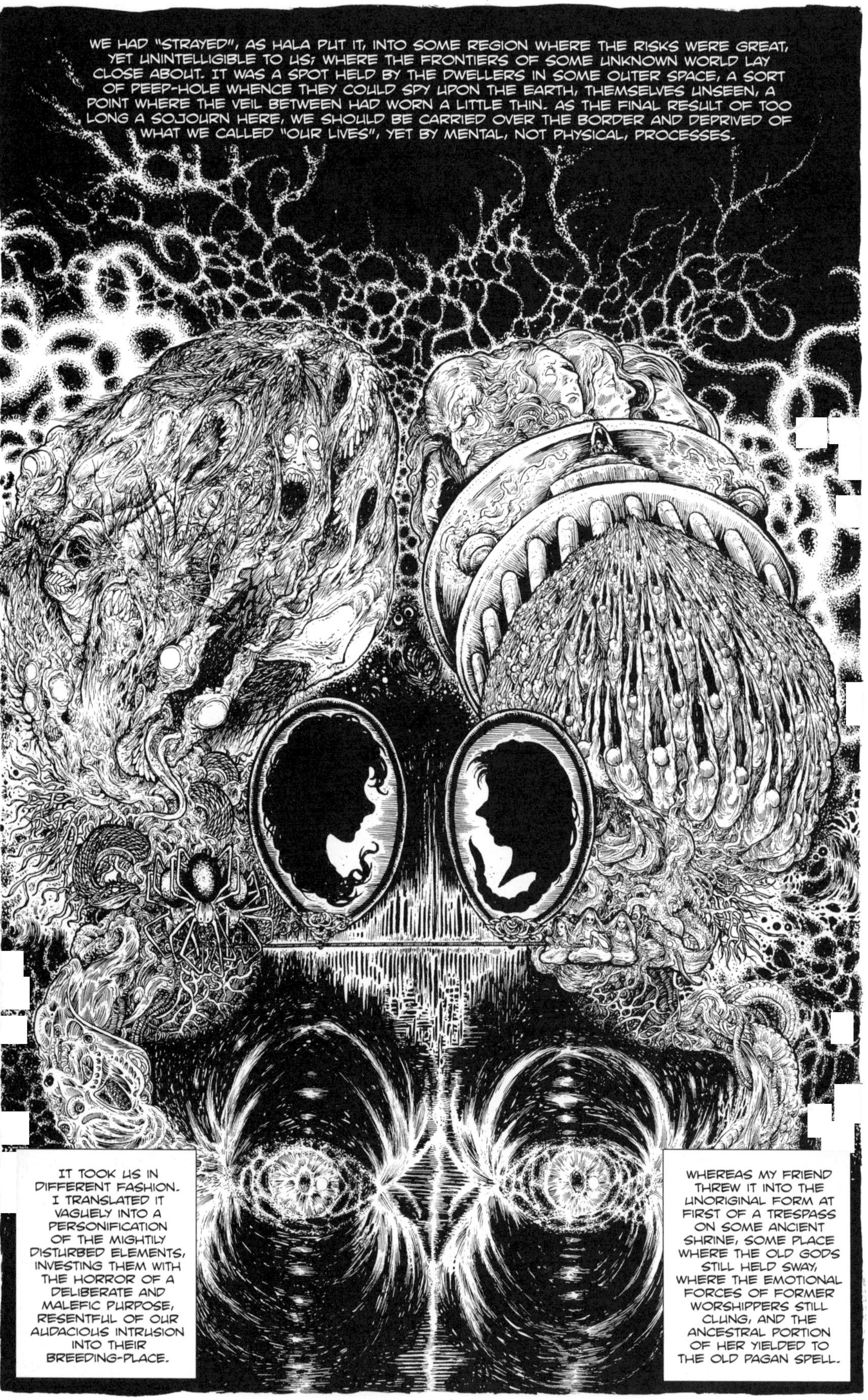
WE HAD "STRAYED", AS HALA PUT IT, INTO SOME REGION WHERE THE RISKS WERE GREAT, YET UNINTELLIGIBLE TO US; WHERE THE FRONTIERS OF SOME UNKNOWN WORLD LAY CLOSE ABOUT. IT WAS A SPOT HELD BY THE DWELLERS IN SOME OUTER SPACE, A SORT OF PEEP-HOLE WHENCE THEY COULD SPY UPON THE EARTH, THEMSELVES UNSEEN, A POINT WHERE THE VEIL BETWEEN HAD WORN A LITTLE THIN. AS THE FINAL RESULT OF TOO LONG A SOJOURN HERE, WE SHOULD BE CARRIED OVER THE BORDER AND DEPRIVED OF WHAT WE CALLED "OUR LIVES", YET BY MENTAL, NOT PHYSICAL, PROCESSES.
IT TOOK US IN DIFFERENT FASHION. I TRANSLATED IT VAGUELY INTO A PERSONIFICATION OF THE MIGHTILY DISTURBED ELEMENTS, INVESTING THEM WITH THE HORROR OF A DELIBERATE AND MALEFIC PURPOSE, RESENTFUL OF OUR AUDACIOUS INTRUSION INTO THEIR BREEDING-PLACE.
WHEREAS MY FRIEND THREW IT INTO THE UNORIGINAL FORM AT FIRST OF A TRESPASS ON SOME ANCIENT SHRINE, SOME PLACE WHERE THE OLD GODS STILL HELD SWAY, WHERE THE EMOTIONAL FORCES OF FORMER WORSHIPPERS STILL CLUNG, AND THE ANCESTRAL PORTION OF HER YIELDED TO THE OLD PAGAN SPELL.

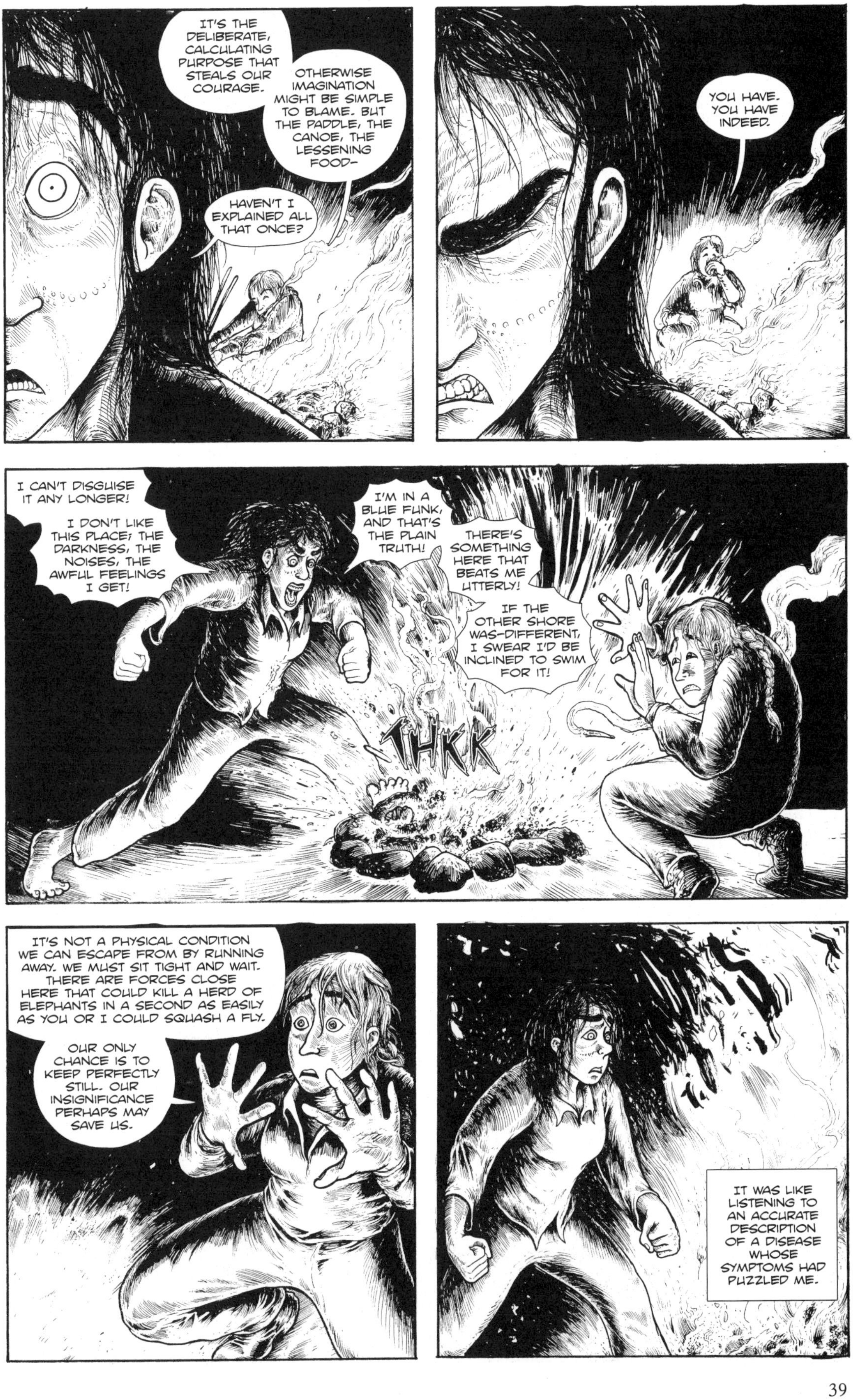
IT'S THE DELIBERATE, CALCULATING PURPOSE THAT STEALS OUR COURAGE.
OTHERWISE IMAGINATION MIGHT BE SIMPLE TO BLAME. BUT THE PADDLE, THE CANOE, THE LESSENING FOOD–
HAVEN'T I EXPLAINED ALL THAT ONCE?
YOU HAVE. YOU HAVE INDEED.
I CAN'T DISGUISE IT ANY LONGER!
I DON'T LIKE THIS PLACE; THE DARKNESS, THE NOISES, THE AWFUL FEELINGS I GET!
I'M IN A BLUE FUNK, AND THAT'S THE PLAIN TRUTH!
THERE'S SOMETHING HERE THAT BEATS ME UTTERLY!
IF THE OTHER SHORE WAS–DIFFERENT, I SWEAR I'D BE INCLINED TO SWIM FOR IT!
THKK
IT'S NOT A PHYSICAL CONDITION WE CAN ESCAPE FROM BY RUNNING AWAY. WE MUST SIT TIGHT AND WAIT. THERE ARE FORCES CLOSE HERE THAT COULD KILL A HERD OF ELEPHANTS IN A SECOND AS EASILY AS YOU OR I COULD SQUASH A FLY.
OUR ONLY CHANCE IS TO KEEP PERFECTLY STILL. OUR INSIGNIFICANCE PERHAPS MAY SAVE US.
IT WAS LIKE LISTENING TO AN ACCURATE DESCRIPTION OF A DISEASE WHOSE SYMPTOMS HAD PUZZLED ME.

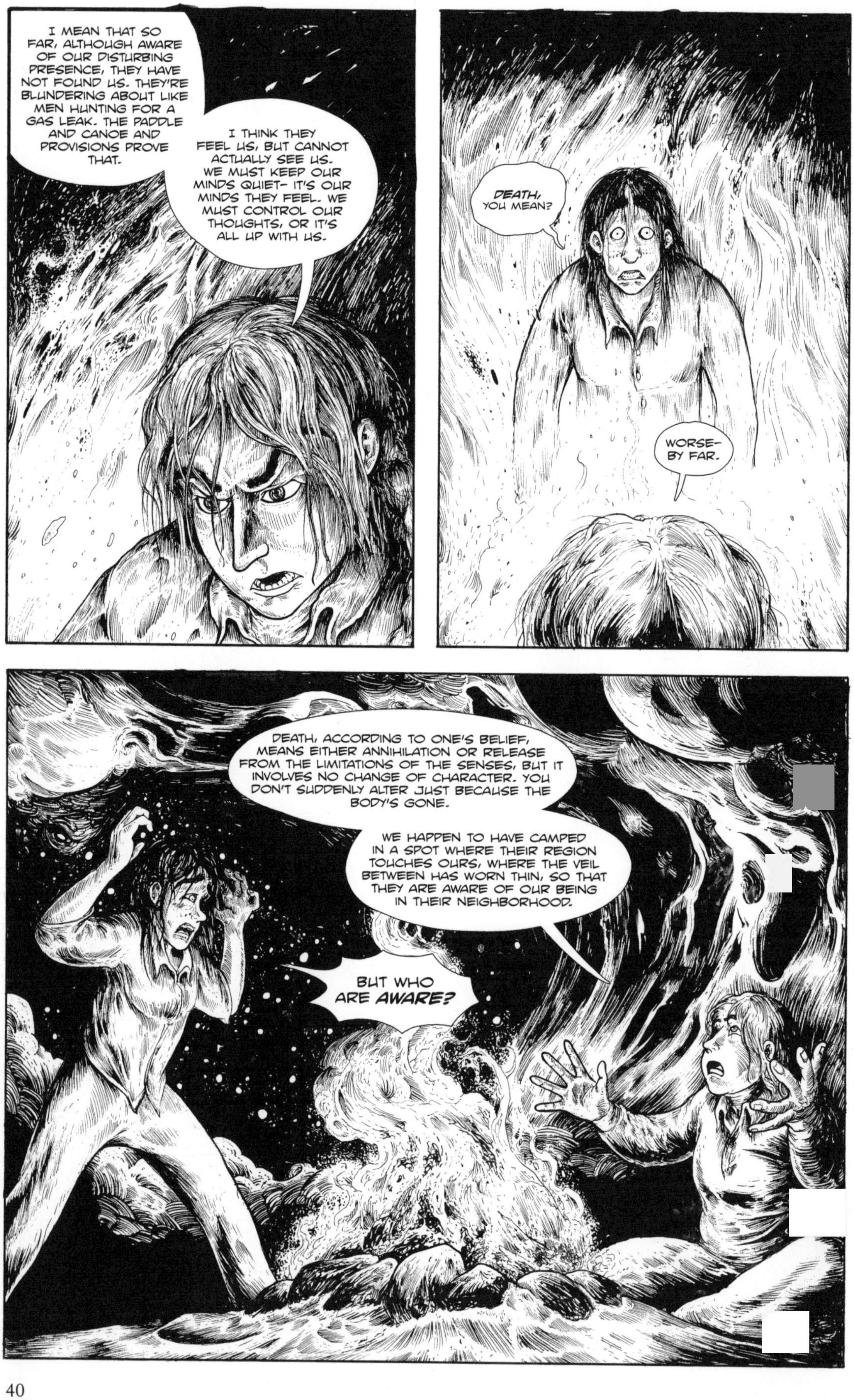

I MEAN THAT SO FAR, ALTHOUGH AWARE OF OUR DISTURBING PRESENCE, THEY HAVE NOT FOUND US. THEY'RE BLUNDERING ABOUT LIKE MEN HUNTING FOR A GAS LEAK. THE PADDLE AND CANOE AND PROVISIONS PROVE THAT.
I THINK THEY FEEL US, BUT CANNOT ACTUALLY SEE US. WE MUST KEEP OUR MINDS QUIET- IT'S OUR MINDS THEY FEEL. WE MUST CONTROL OUR THOUGHTS, OR IT'S ALL UP WITH US.
DEATH, YOU MEAN?
WORSE- BY FAR.
DEATH, ACCORDING TO ONE'S BELIEF, MEANS EITHER ANNIHILATION OR RELEASE FROM THE LIMITATIONS OF THE SENSES, BUT IT INVOLVES NO CHANGE OF CHARACTER. YOU DON'T SUDDENLY ALTER JUST BECAUSE THE BODY'S GONE.
WE HAPPEN TO HAVE CAMPED IN A SPOT WHERE THEIR REGION TOUCHES OURS, WHERE THE VEIL BETWEEN HAS WORN THIN, SO THAT THEY ARE AWARE OF OUR BEING IN THEIR NEIGHBORHOOD.
BUT WHO ARE AWARE?

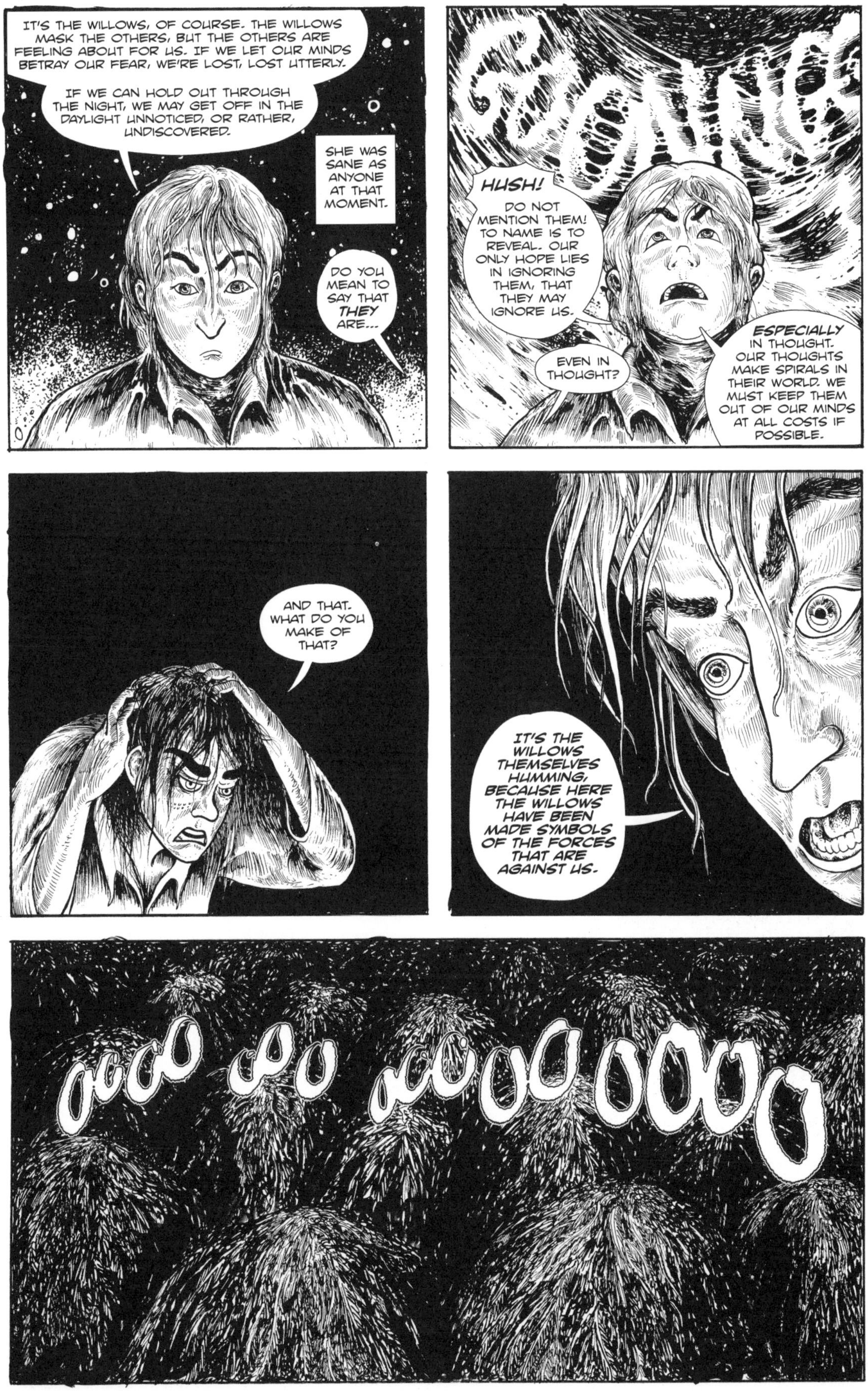
IT'S THE WILLOWS, OF COURSE. THE WILLOWS MASK THE OTHERS, BUT THE OTHERS ARE FEELING ABOUT FOR US. IF WE LET OUR MINDS BETRAY OUR FEAR, WE'RE LOST, LOST UTTERLY.
IF WE CAN HOLD OUT THROUGH THE NIGHT, WE MAY GET OFF IN THE DAYLIGHT UNNOTICED, OR RATHER, UNDISCOVERED.
SHE WAS SANE AS ANYONE AT THAT MOMENT.
DO YOU MEAN TO SAY THAT THEY ARE...
HUSH! DO NOT MENTION THEM! TO NAME IS TO REVEAL. OUR ONLY HOPE LIES IN IGNORING THEM, THAT THEY MAY IGNORE US.
EVEN IN THOUGHT?
ESPECIALLY IN THOUGHT. OUR THOUGHTS MAKE SPIRALS IN THEIR WORLD. WE MUST KEEP THEM OUT OF OUR MINDS AT ALL COSTS IF POSSIBLE.
AND THAT. WHAT DO YOU MAKE OF THAT?
IT'S THE WILLOWS THEMSELVES HUMMING, BECAUSE HERE THE WILLOWS HAVE BEEN MADE SYMBOLS OF THE FORCES THAT ARE AGAINST US.

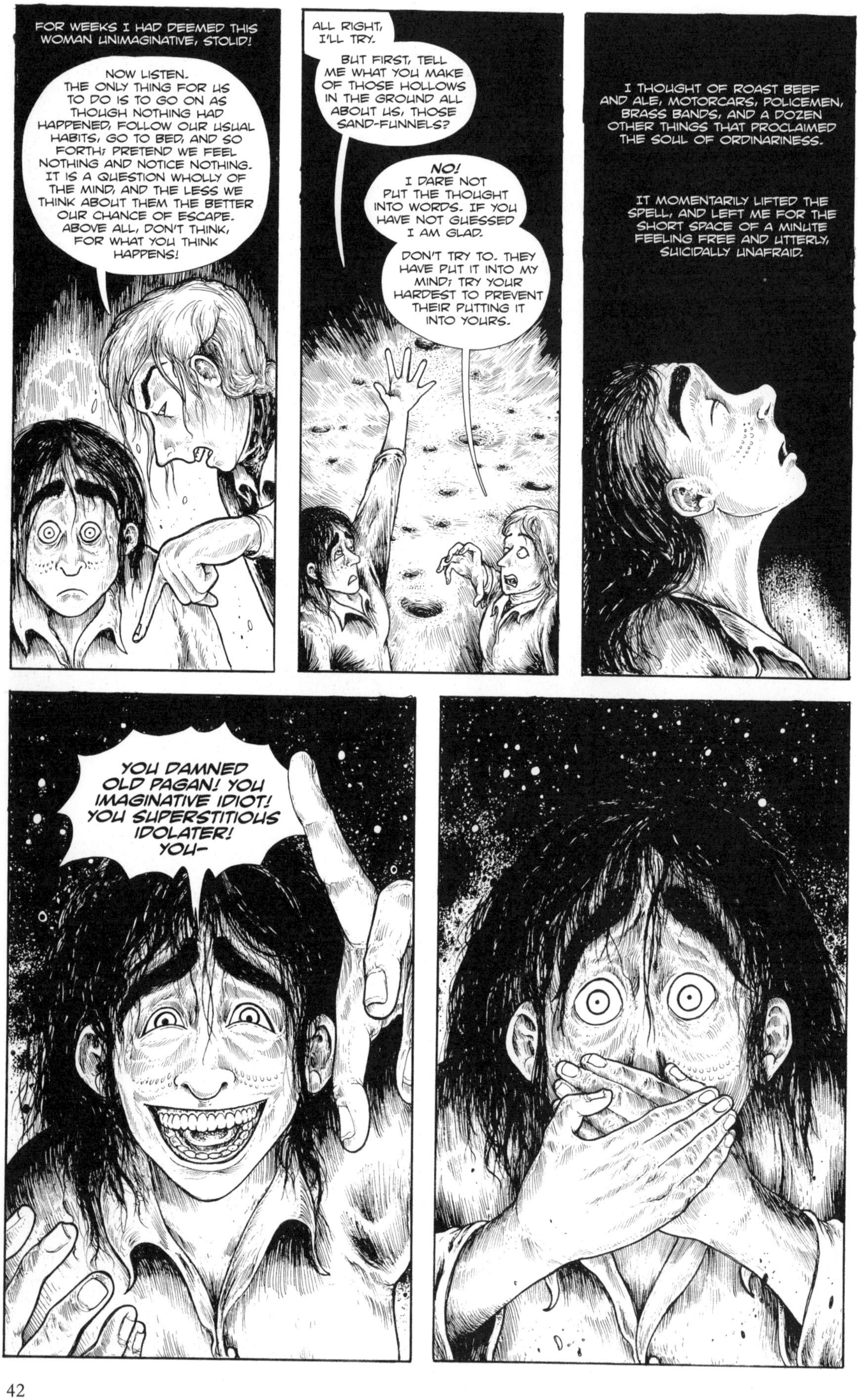

FOR WEEKS I HAD DEEMED THIS WOMAN UNIMAGINATIVE, STOLID!
NOW LISTEN. THE ONLY THING FOR US TO DO IS TO GO ON AS THOUGH NOTHING HAD HAPPENED, FOLLOW OUR USUAL HABITS, GO TO BED, AND SO FORTH; PRETEND WE FEEL NOTHING AND NOTICE NOTHING. IT IS A QUESTION WHOLLY OF THE MIND, AND THE LESS WE THINK ABOUT THEM THE BETTER OUR CHANCE OF ESCAPE. ABOVE ALL, DON'T THINK, FOR WHAT YOU THINK HAPPENS!
ALL RIGHT, I'LL TRY.
BUT FIRST, TELL ME WHAT YOU MAKE OF THOSE HOLLOWS IN THE GROUND ALL ABOUT US, THOSE SAND-FUNNELS?
NO! I DARE NOT PUT THE THOUGHT INTO WORDS. IF YOU HAVE NOT GUESSED I AM GLAD.
DON'T TRY TO. THEY HAVE PUT IT INTO MY MIND; TRY YOUR HARDEST TO PREVENT THEIR PUTTING IT INTO YOURS.
I THOUGHT OF ROAST BEEF AND ALE, MOTORCARS, POLICEMEN, BRASS BANDS, AND A DOZEN OTHER THINGS THAT PROCLAIMED THE SOUL OF ORDINARINESS.
IT MOMENTARILY LIFTED THE SPELL, AND LEFT ME FOR THE SHORT SPACE OF A MINUTE FEELING FREE AND UTTERLY, SUICIDALLY UNAFRAID.
YOU DAMNED OLD PAGAN! YOU IMAGINATIVE IDIOT! YOU SUPERSTITIOUS IDOLATER! YOU-

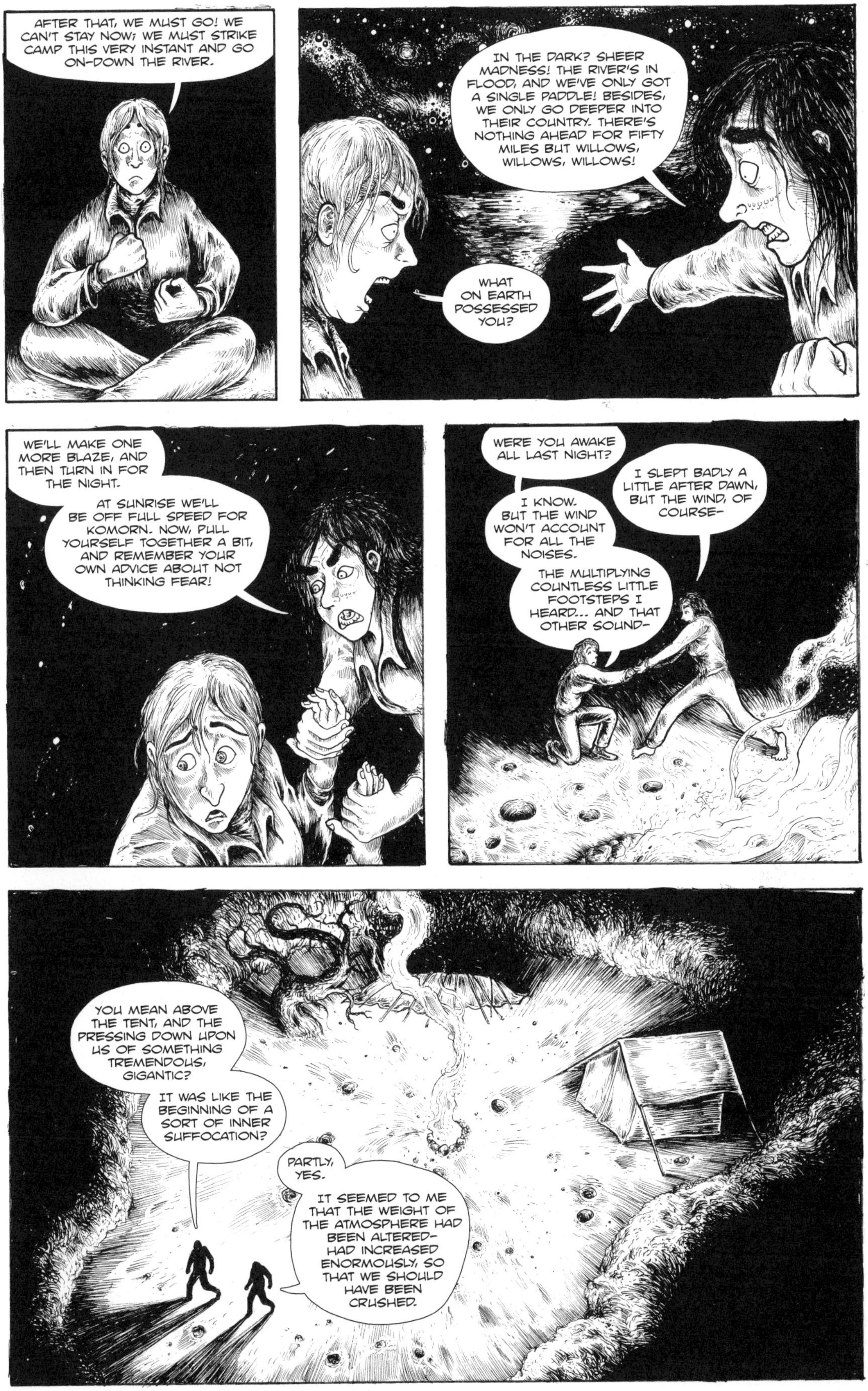
AFTER THAT, WE MUST GO! WE CAN'T STAY NOW; WE MUST STRIKE CAMP THIS VERY INSTANT AND GO ON-DOWN THE RIVER.
IN THE DARK? SHEER MADNESS! THE RIVER'S IN FLOOD, AND WE'VE ONLY GOT A SINGLE PADDLE! BESIDES, WE ONLY GO DEEPER INTO THEIR COUNTRY. THERE'S NOTHING AHEAD FOR FIFTY MILES BUT WILLOWS, WILLOWS, WILLOWS!
WHAT ON EARTH POSSESSED YOU?
WE'LL MAKE ONE MORE BLAZE, AND THEN TURN IN FOR THE NIGHT.
AT SUNRISE WE'LL BE OFF FULL SPEED FOR KOMORN. NOW, PULL YOURSELF TOGETHER A BIT, AND REMEMBER YOUR OWN ADVICE ABOUT NOT THINKING FEAR!
WERE YOU AWAKE ALL LAST NIGHT?
I SLEPT BADLY A LITTLE AFTER DAWN, BUT THE WIND, OF COURSE-
I KNOW. BUT THE WIND WON'T ACCOUNT FOR ALL THE NOISES.
THE MULTIPLYING COUNTLESS LITTLE FOOTSTEPS I HEARD... AND THAT OTHER SOUND-
YOU MEAN ABOVE THE TENT, AND THE PRESSING DOWN UPON US OF SOMETHING TREMENDOUS, GIGANTIC?
IT WAS LIKE THE BEGINNING OF A SORT OF INNER SUFFOCATION?
PARTLY, YES.
IT SEEMED TO ME THAT THE WEIGHT OF THE ATMOSPHERE HAD BEEN ALTERED- HAD INCREASED ENORMOUSLY, SO THAT WE SHOULD HAVE BEEN CRUSHED.

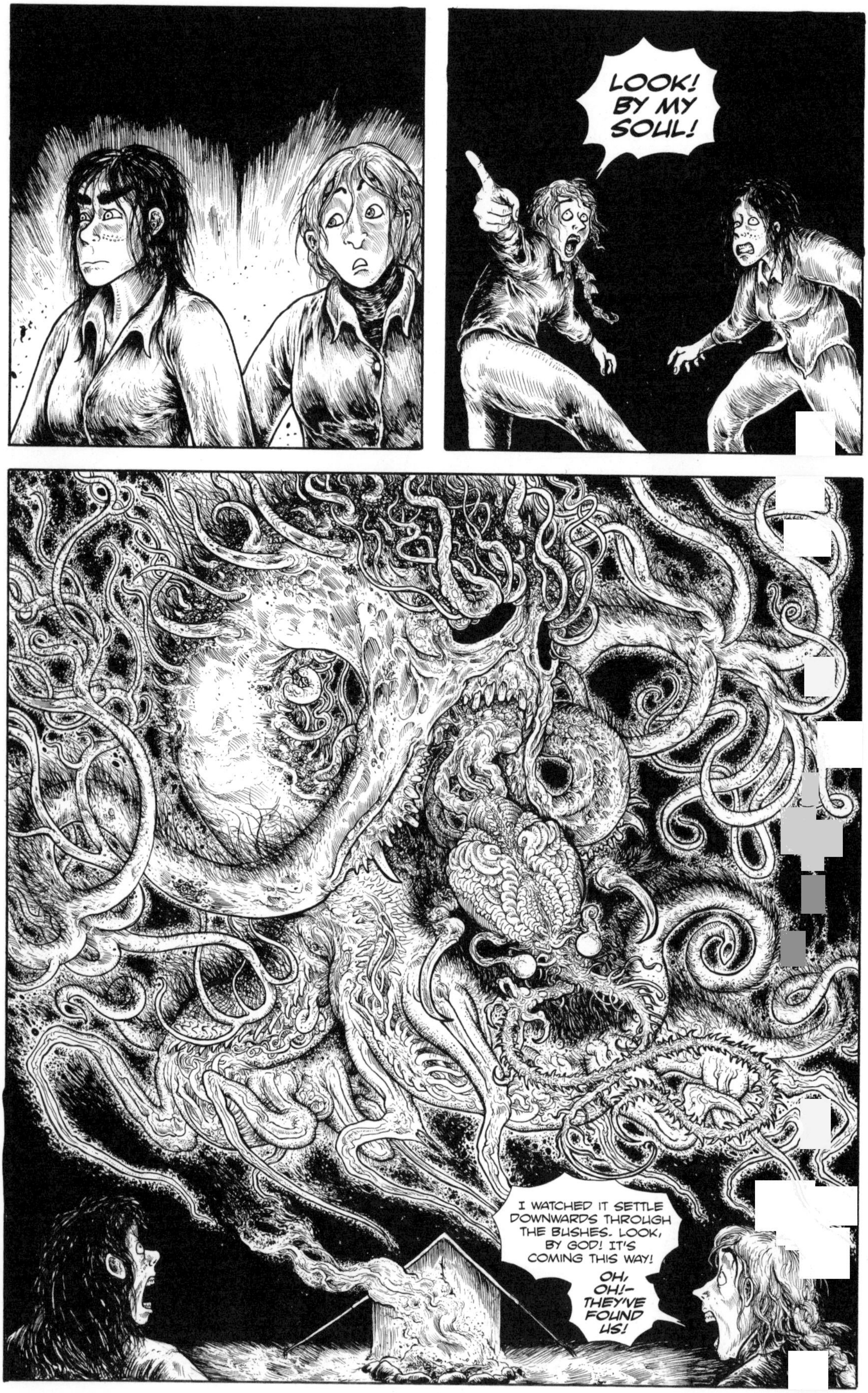
LOOK! BY MY SOUL!
I WATCHED IT SETTLE DOWNWARDS THROUGH THE BUSHES. LOOK, BY GOD! IT'S COMING THIS WAY!
OH, OH!- THEY'VE FOUND US!

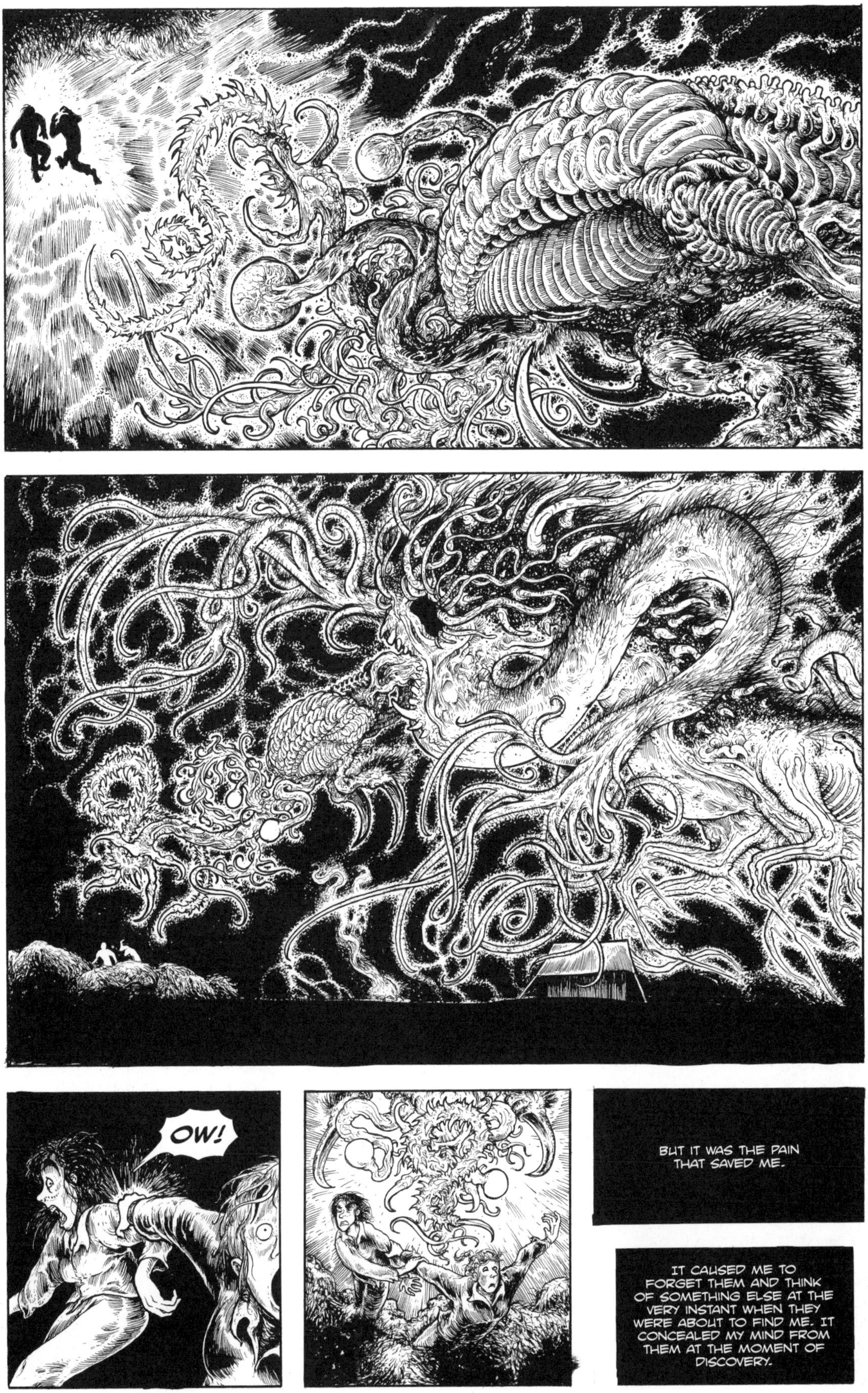
OW!
BUT IT WAS THE PAIN THAT SAVED ME.
IT CAUSED ME TO FORGET THEM AND THINK OF SOMETHING ELSE AT THE VERY INSTANT WHEN THEY WERE ABOUT TO FIND ME. IT CONCEALED MY MIND FROM THEM AT THE MOMENT OF DISCOVERY.

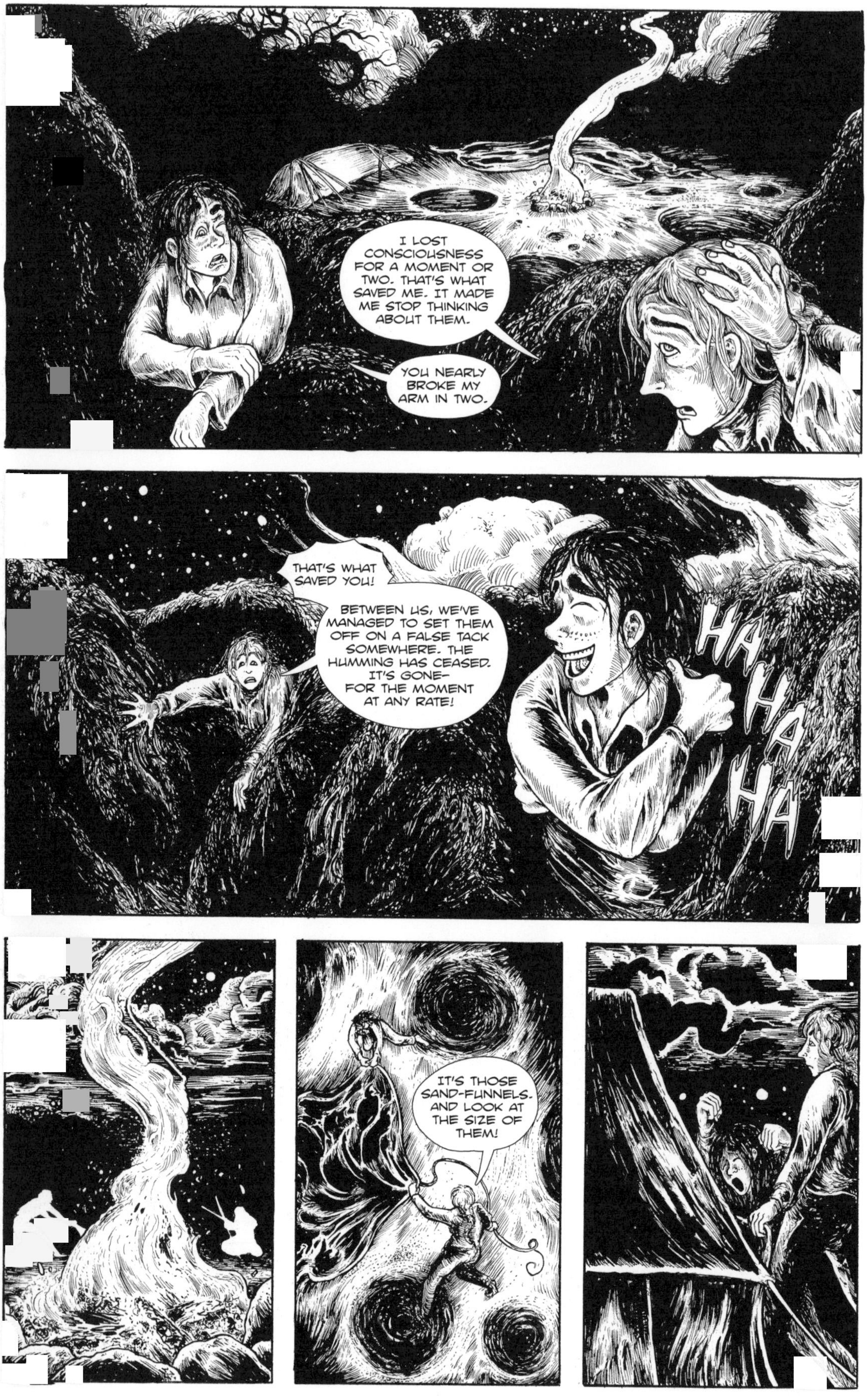
I LOST CONSCIOUSNESS FOR A MOMENT OR TWO. THAT'S WHAT SAVED ME. IT MADE ME STOP THINKING ABOUT THEM.
YOU NEARLY BROKE MY ARM IN TWO.
THAT'S WHAT SAVED YOU!
BETWEEN US, WE'VE MANAGED TO SET THEM OFF ON A FALSE TACK SOMEWHERE. THE HUMMING HAS CEASED. IT'S GONE— FOR THE MOMENT AT ANY RATE!
HA HA HA HA
IT'S THOSE SAND-FUNNELS. AND LOOK AT THE SIZE OF THEM!

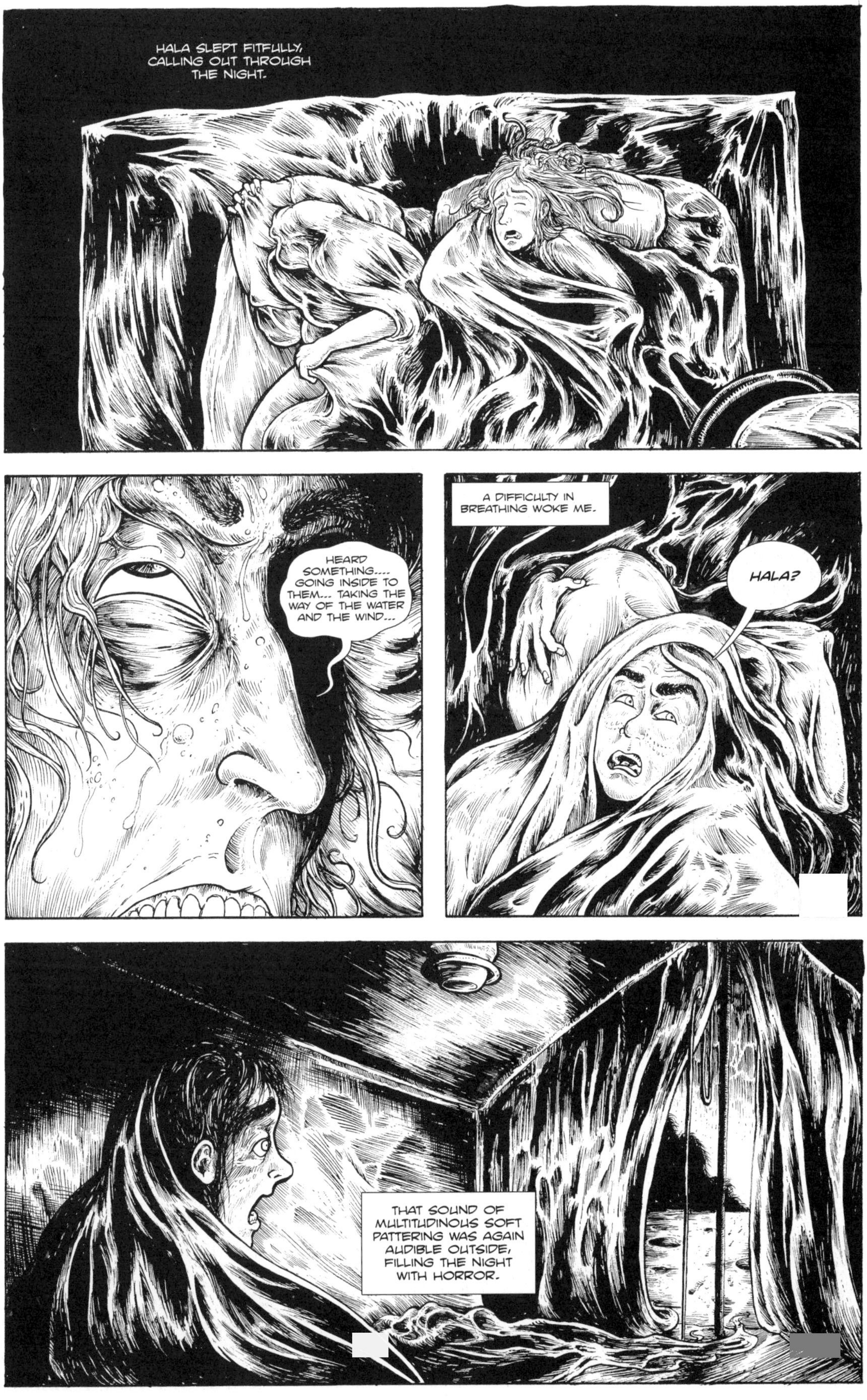

HALA SLEPT FITFULLY, CALLING OUT THROUGH THE NIGHT.
HEARD SOMETHING.... GOING INSIDE TO THEM... TAKING THE WAY OF THE WATER AND THE WIND...
A DIFFICULTY IN BREATHING WOKE ME.
HALA?
THAT SOUND OF MULTITUDINOUS SOFT PATTERING WAS AGAIN AUDIBLE OUTSIDE, FILLING THE NIGHT WITH HORROR.

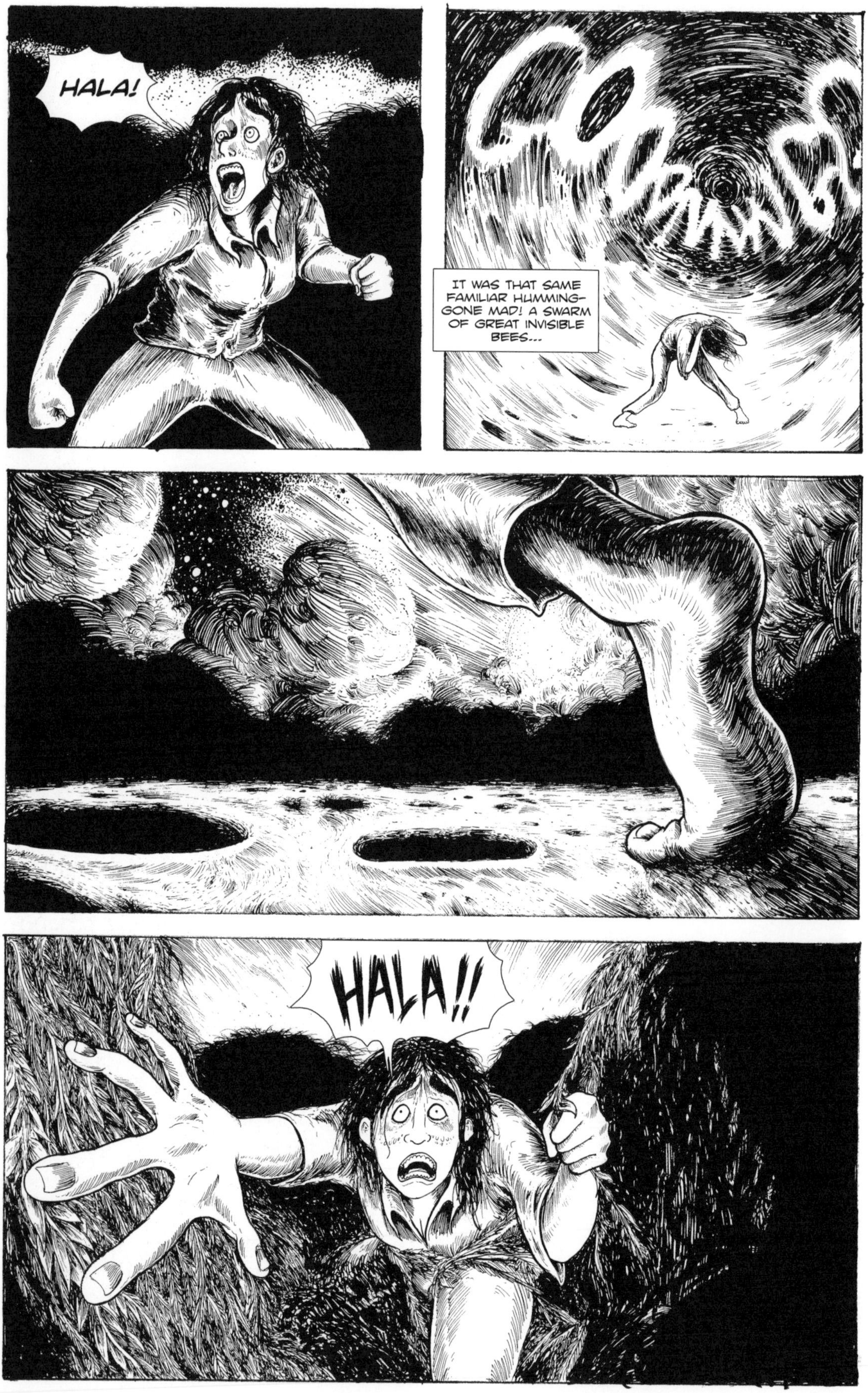
HALA!
IT WAS THAT SAME FAMILIAR HUMMING- GONE MAD! A SWARM OF GREAT INVISIBLE BEES...
HALA!!

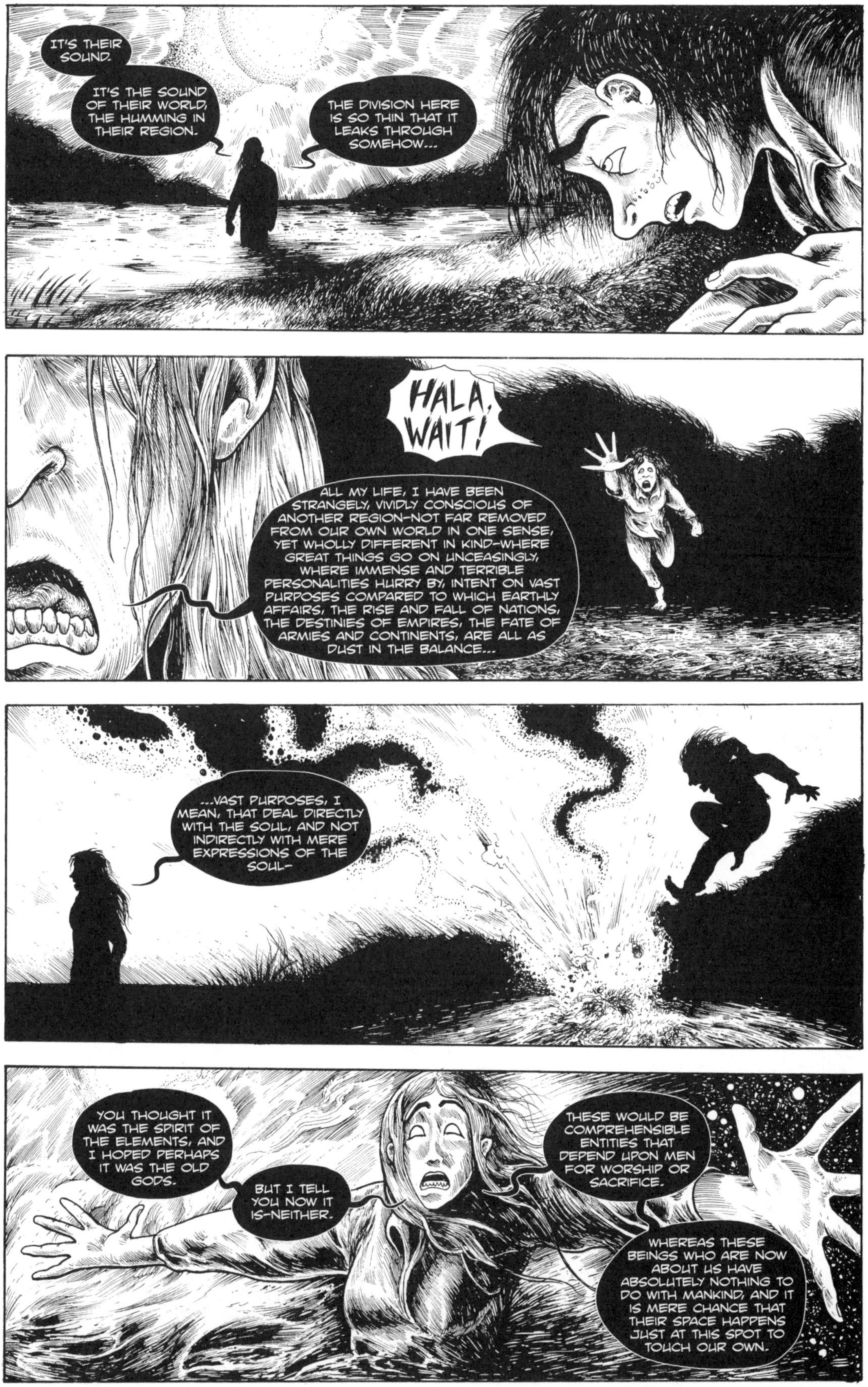
IT'S THEIR SOUND.
IT'S THE SOUND OF THEIR WORLD, THE HUMMING IN THEIR REGION.
THE DIVISION HERE IS SO THIN THAT IT LEAKS THROUGH SOMEHOW...
HALA, WAIT!
ALL MY LIFE, I HAVE BEEN STRANGELY, VIVIDLY CONSCIOUS OF ANOTHER REGION-NOT FAR REMOVED FROM OUR OWN WORLD IN ONE SENSE, YET WHOLLY DIFFERENT IN KIND-WHERE GREAT THINGS GO ON UNCEASINGLY, WHERE IMMENSE AND TERRIBLE PERSONALITIES HURRY BY, INTENT ON VAST PURPOSES COMPARED TO WHICH EARTHLY AFFAIRS, THE RISE AND FALL OF NATIONS, THE DESTINIES OF EMPIRES, THE FATE OF ARMIES AND CONTINENTS, ARE ALL AS DUST IN THE BALANCE...
...VAST PURPOSES, I MEAN, THAT DEAL DIRECTLY WITH THE SOUL, AND NOT INDIRECTLY WITH MERE EXPRESSIONS OF THE SOUL-
YOU THOUGHT IT WAS THE SPIRIT OF THE ELEMENTS, AND I HOPED PERHAPS IT WAS THE OLD GODS.
BUT I TELL YOU NOW IT IS-NEITHER.
THESE WOULD BE COMPREHENSIBLE ENTITIES THAT DEPEND UPON MEN FOR WORSHIP OR SACRIFICE.
WHEREAS THESE BEINGS WHO ARE NOW ABOUT US HAVE ABSOLUTELY NOTHING TO DO WITH MANKIND, AND IT IS MERE CHANCE THAT THEIR SPACE HAPPENS JUST AT THIS SPOT TO TOUCH OUR OWN.

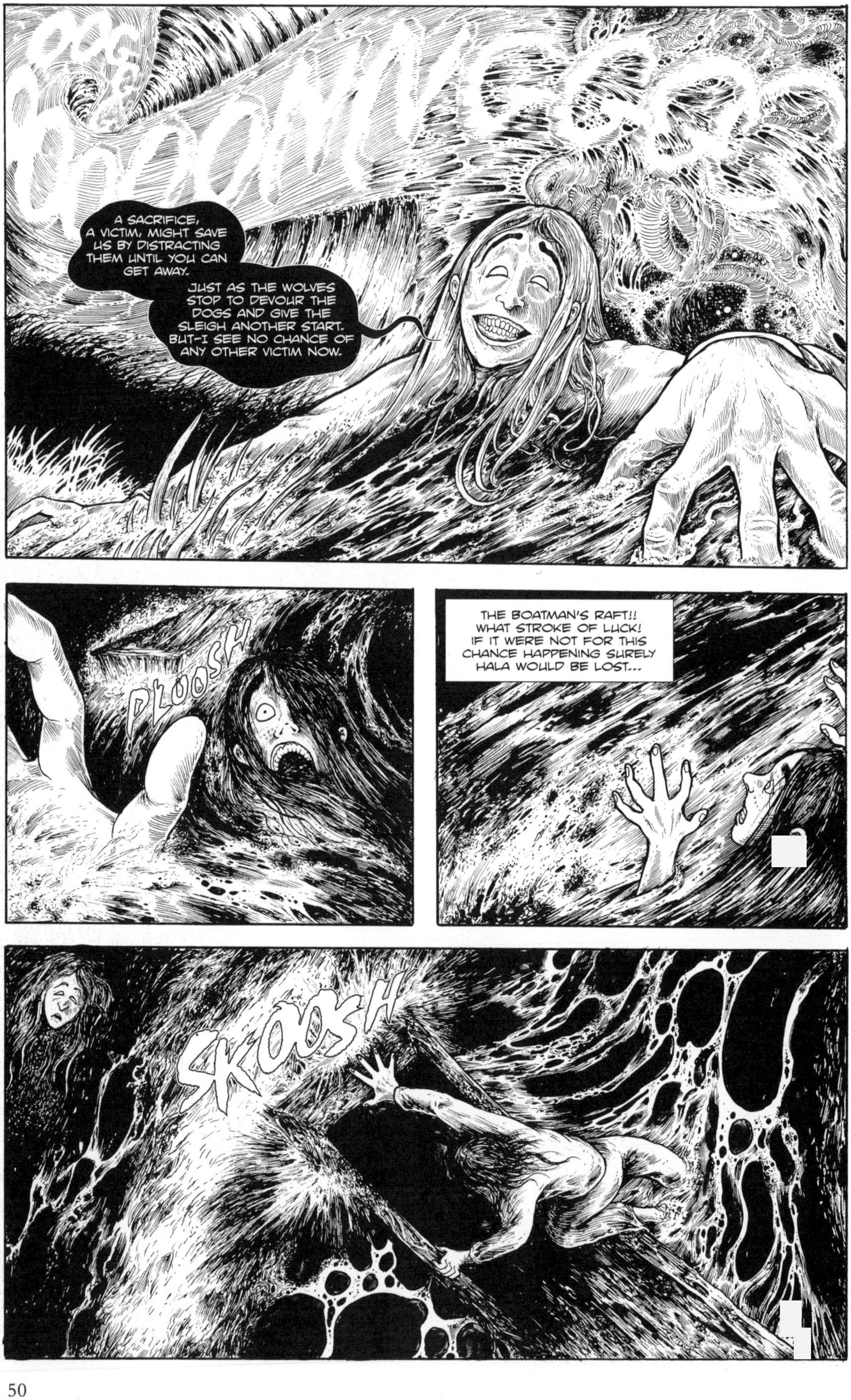
A SACRIFICE, A VICTIM, MIGHT SAVE US BY DISTRACTING THEM UNTIL YOU CAN GET AWAY.
JUST AS THE WOLVES STOP TO DEVOUR THE DOGS AND GIVE THE SLEIGH ANOTHER START. BUT--I SEE NO CHANCE OF ANY OTHER VICTIM NOW.
PLOOSH
THE BOATMAN'S RAFT!! WHAT STROKE OF LUCK! IF IT WERE NOT FOR THIS CHANCE HAPPENING SURELY HALA WOULD BE LOST...
SKOOSH

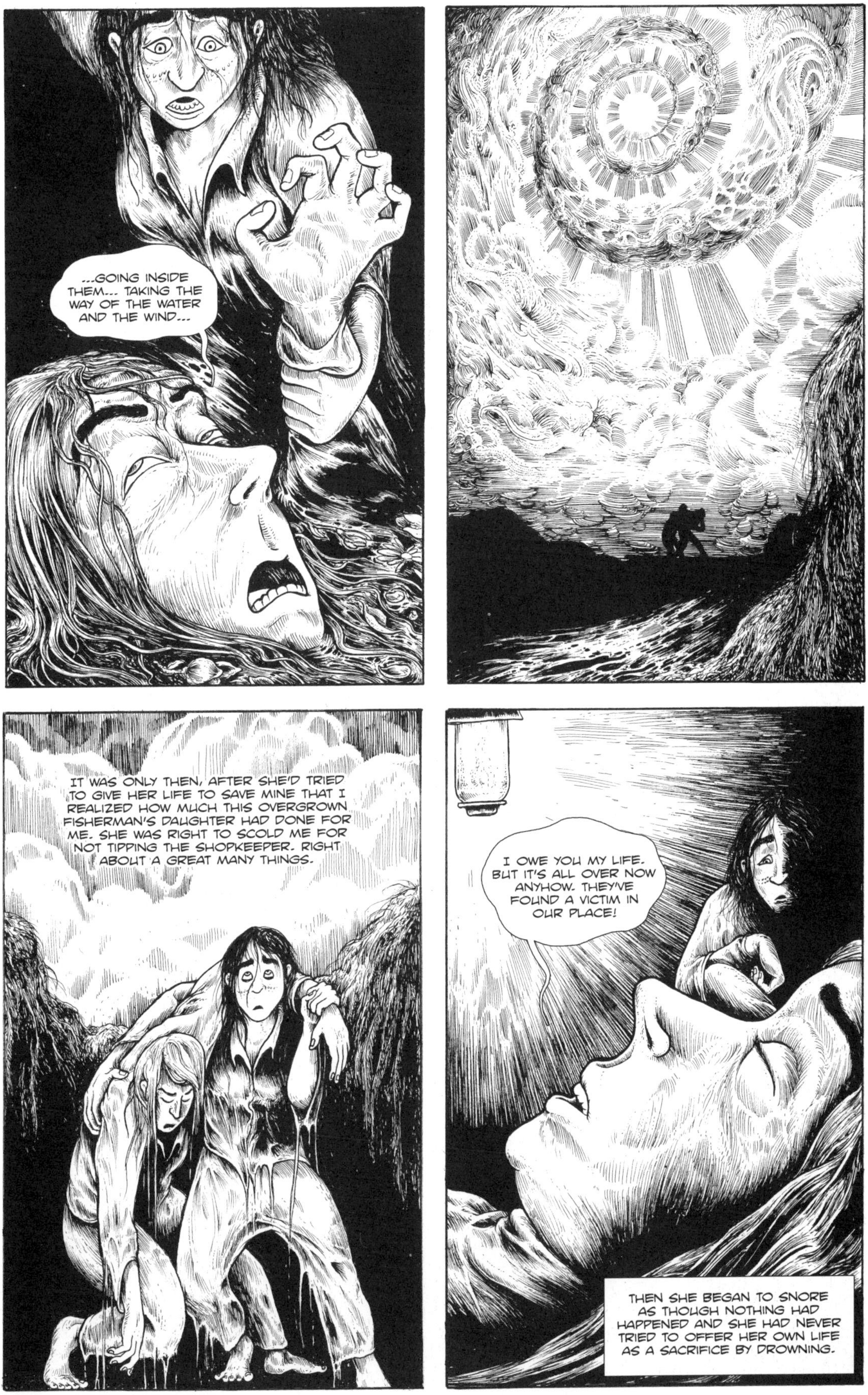
...GOING INSIDE THEM... TAKING THE WAY OF THE WATER AND THE WIND...
IT WAS ONLY THEN, AFTER SHE'D TRIED TO GIVE HER LIFE TO SAVE MINE THAT I REALIZED HOW MUCH THIS OVERGROWN FISHERMAN'S DAUGHTER HAD DONE FOR ME. SHE WAS RIGHT TO SCOLD ME FOR NOT TIPPING THE SHOPKEEPER. RIGHT ABOUT A GREAT MANY THINGS.
I OWE YOU MY LIFE. BUT IT'S ALL OVER NOW ANYHOW. THEY'VE FOUND A VICTIM IN OUR PLACE!
THEN SHE BEGAN TO SNORE AS THOUGH NOTHING HAD HAPPENED AND SHE HAD NEVER TRIED TO OFFER HER OWN LIFE AS A SACRIFICE BY DROWNING.

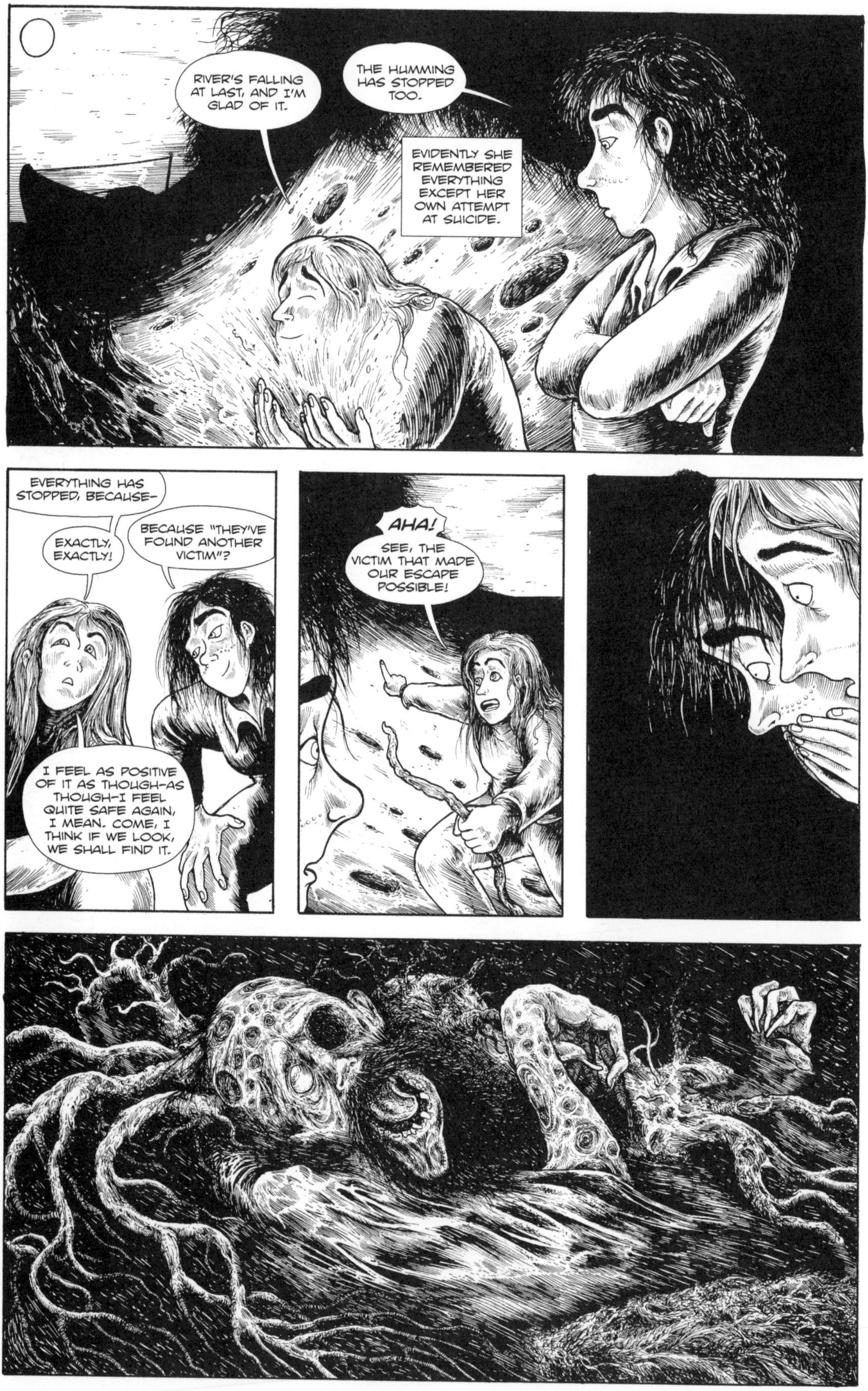

RIVER'S FALLING AT LAST, AND I'M GLAD OF IT.
THE HUMMING HAS STOPPED TOO.
EVIDENTLY SHE REMEMBERED EVERYTHING EXCEPT HER OWN ATTEMPT AT SUICIDE.
EVERYTHING HAS STOPPED, BECAUSE-
EXACTLY, EXACTLY!
BECAUSE "THEY'VE FOUND ANOTHER VICTIM"?
I FEEL AS POSITIVE OF IT AS THOUGH-AS THOUGH-I FEEL QUITE SAFE AGAIN, I MEAN. COME, I THINK IF WE LOOK, WE SHALL FIND IT.
AHA!
SEE, THE VICTIM THAT MADE OUR ESCAPE POSSIBLE!

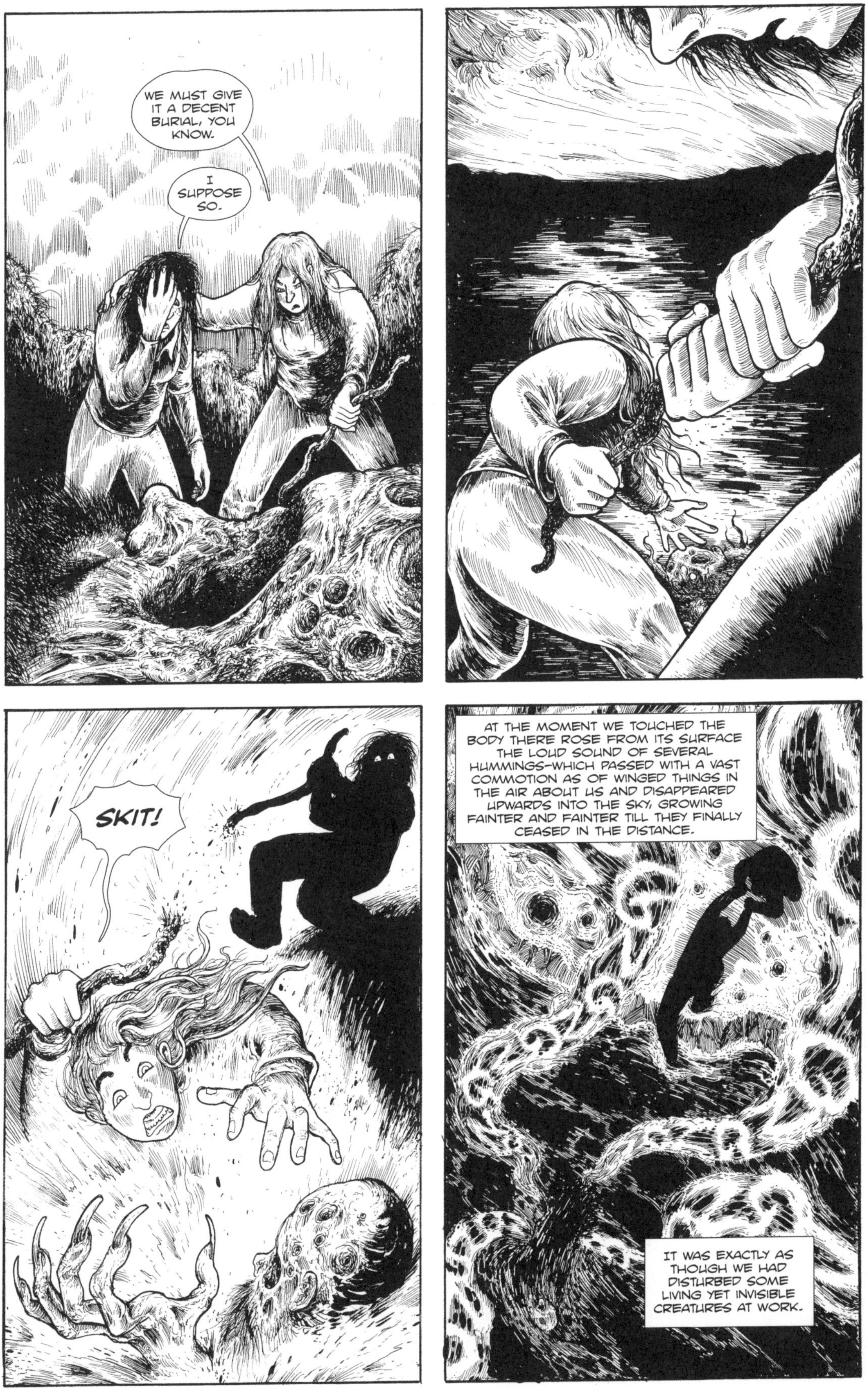
WE MUST GIVE IT A DECENT BURIAL, YOU KNOW.
I SUPPOSE SO.
SKIT!
AT THE MOMENT WE TOUCHED THE BODY THERE ROSE FROM ITS SURFACE THE LOUD SOUND OF SEVERAL HUMMINGS—WHICH PASSED WITH A VAST COMMOTION AS OF WINGED THINGS IN THE AIR ABOUT US AND DISAPPEARED UPWARDS INTO THE SKY, GROWING FAINTER AND FAINTER TILL THEY FINALLY CEASED IN THE DISTANCE.
IT WAS EXACTLY AS THOUGH WE HAD DISTURBED SOME LIVING YET INVISIBLE CREATURES AT WORK.

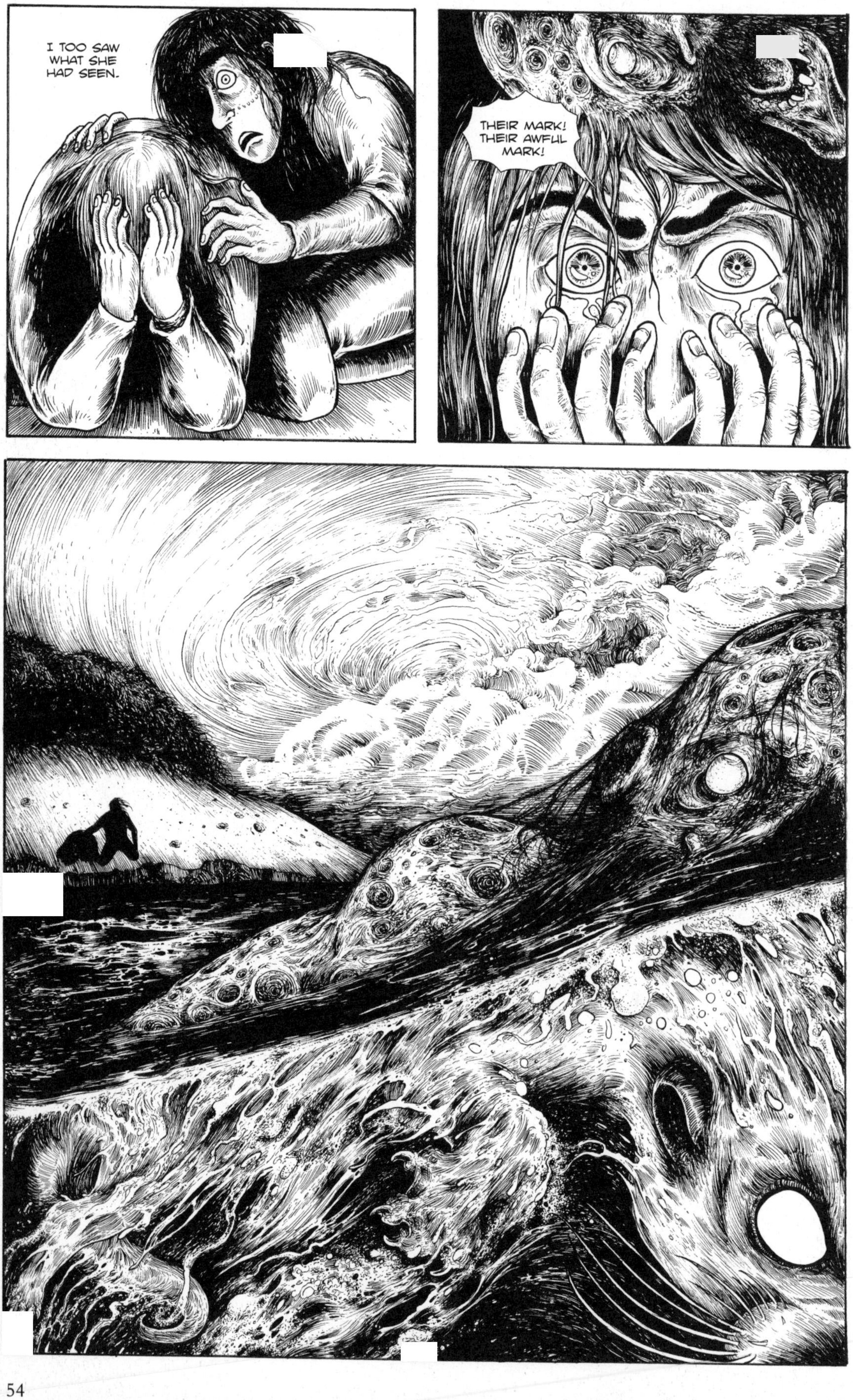
I TOO SAW
WHAT SHE
HAD SEEN.
THEIR MARK!
THEIR AWFUL
MARK!

Hala "The Swede"
Name meaning: Halo
(See also the optical phenomenon.)
Born Sep 6, 1877 (Virgo), Year of the Red Fire Ox.
Age 29

Hala is a stoic Swedish woman in her late twenties. She was raised by her fisherman family and, because of her size and strength, learned to work as hard as the boys. Because of her own intellect and skills, she took a strong interest in equality.

Opal
Name meaning: Dark, black
(Opals are beautiful and valuable gemstones.)
Born Aug 20, 1882 (Leo), Year of the Black Water Horse.
Age 25

Born into Victorian British aristocracy, Opal is nonetheless a wild and free spirit. She was married off young to an older man who left her a sizable inheritance upon his early death. This was Opal's ticket to freedom.

WELL MET IN BOHEMIA

The First of the Continuing Adventures of Opal and Hala

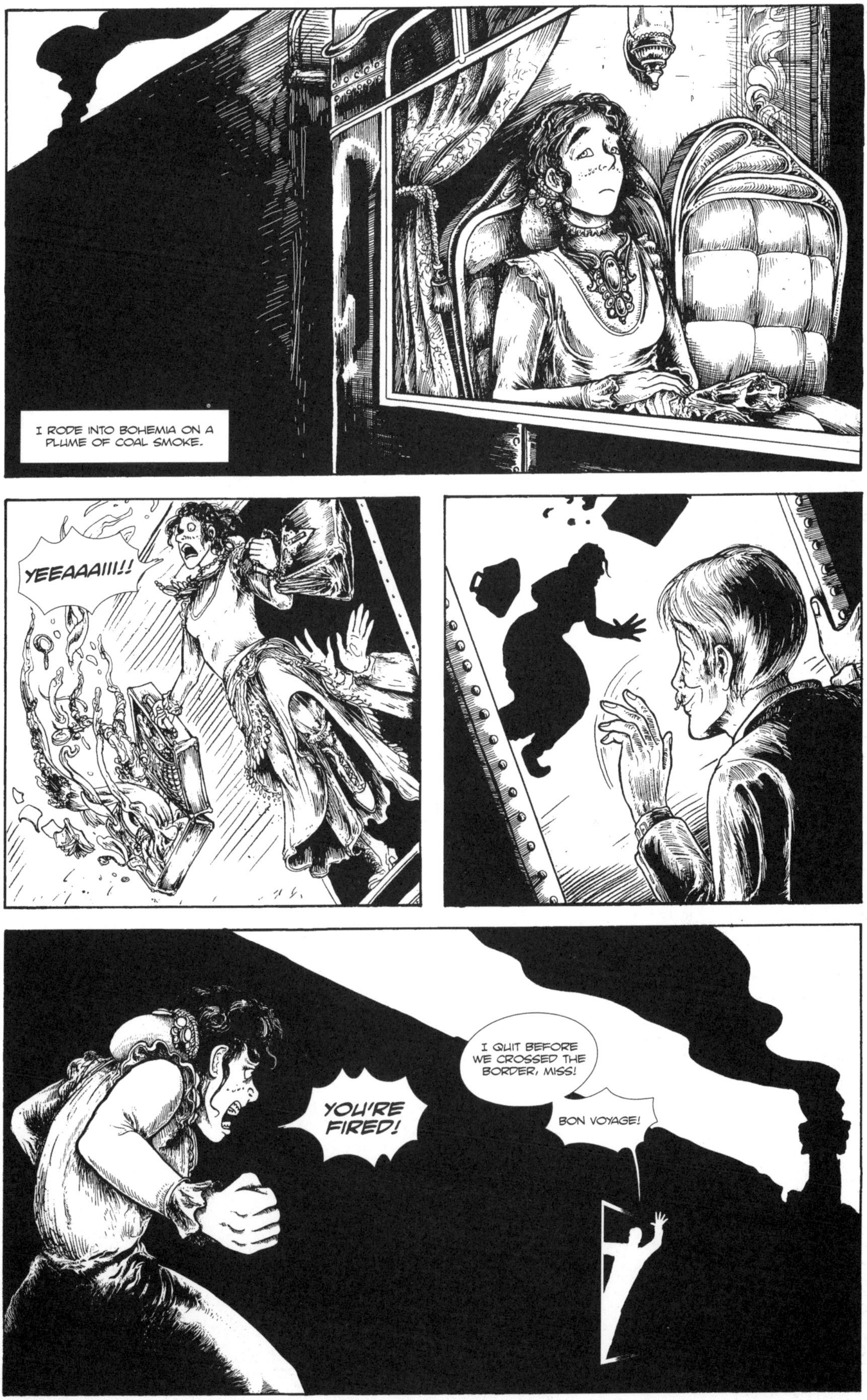

I RODE INTO BOHEMIA ON A PLUME OF COAL SMOKE.
YEEAAAIII!!
YOU'RE FIRED!
I QUIT BEFORE WE CROSSED THE BORDER, MISS!
BON VOYAGE!

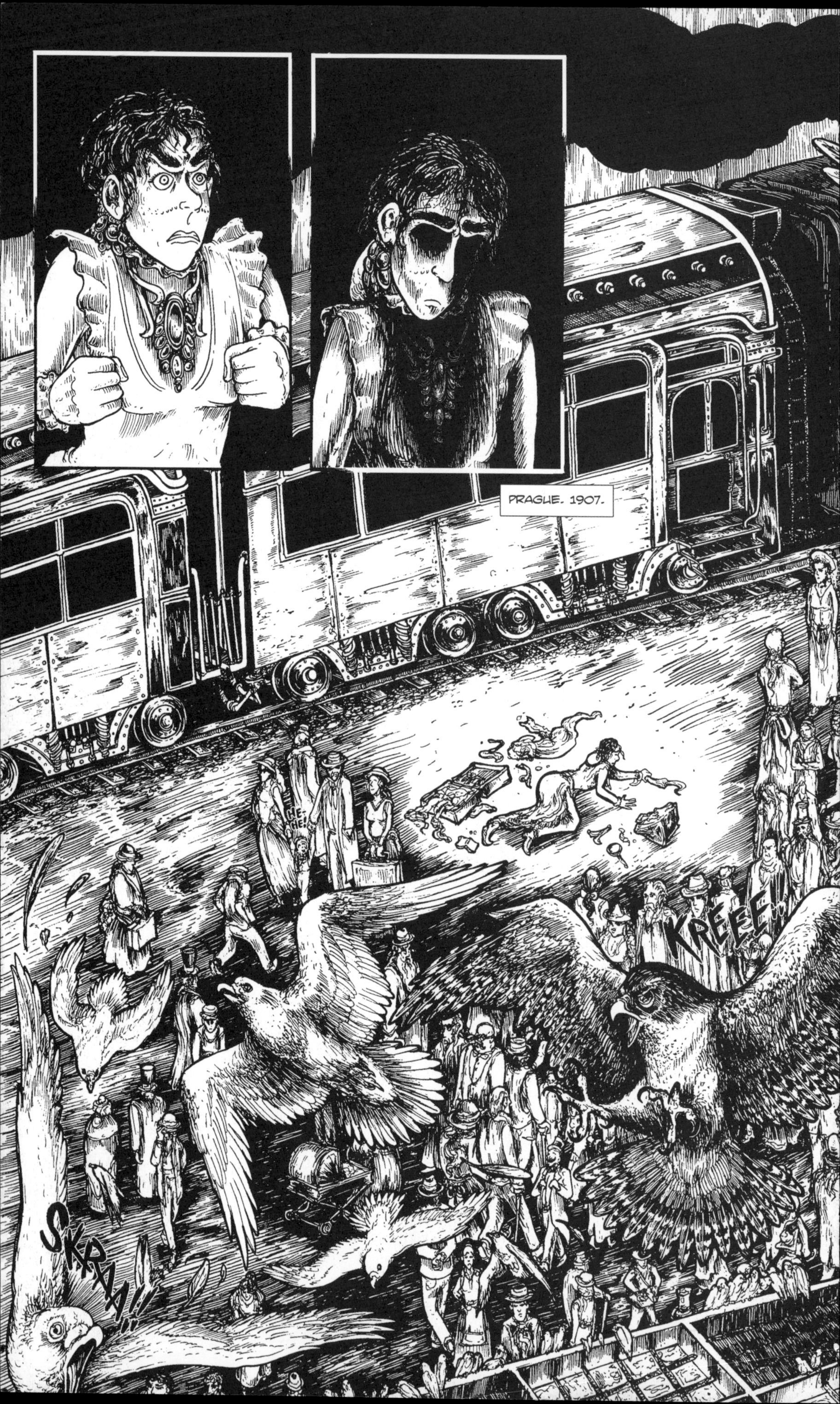

PRAGUE. 1907.
HE HE!
KREEE
SKRAA!!

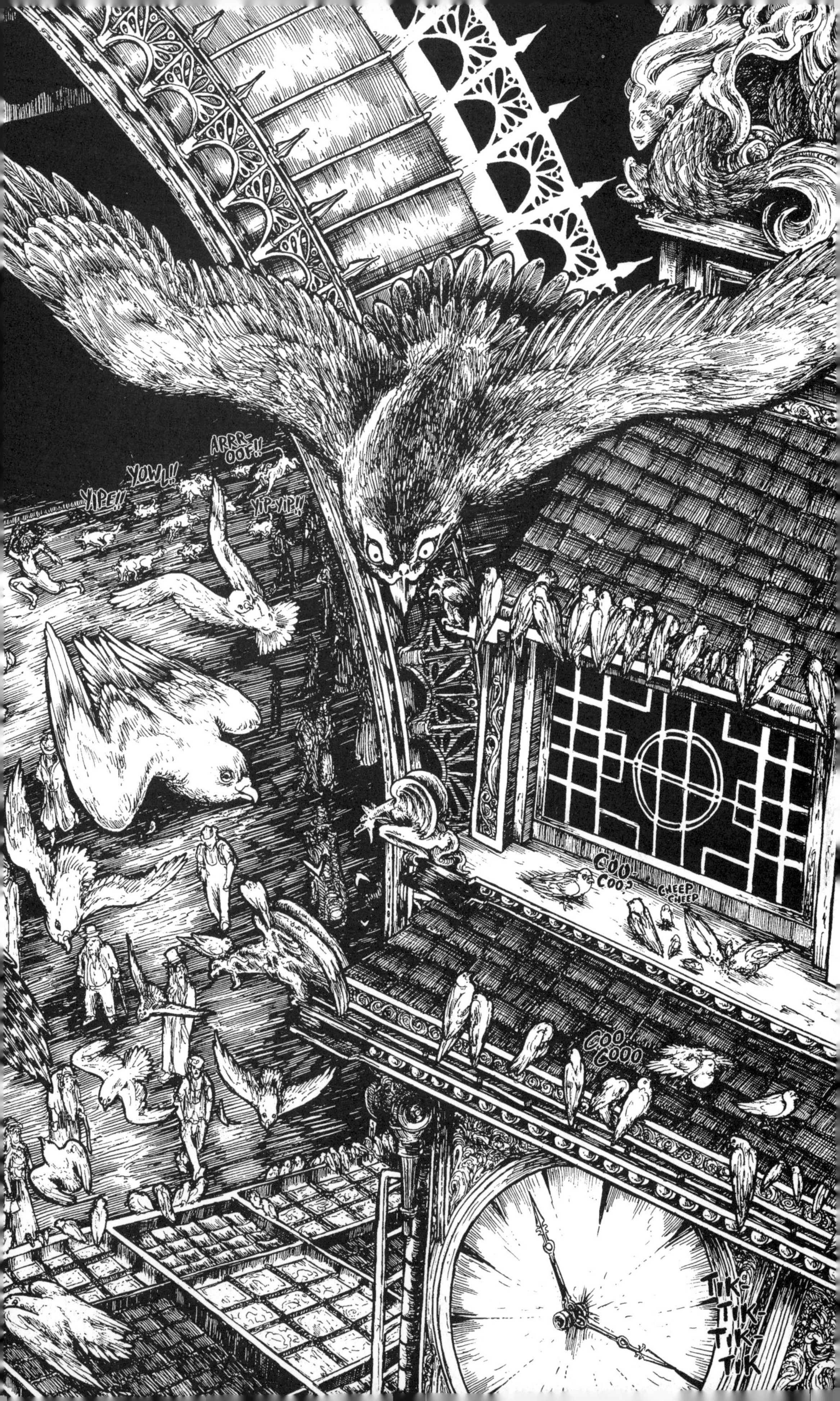

YIPE!!
YOWL!!
ARRR-OOF!!
YIP-YIP!!
COO-COO
CHEEP CHEEP
COO COOO
TIK-TIK-TIK-TIK

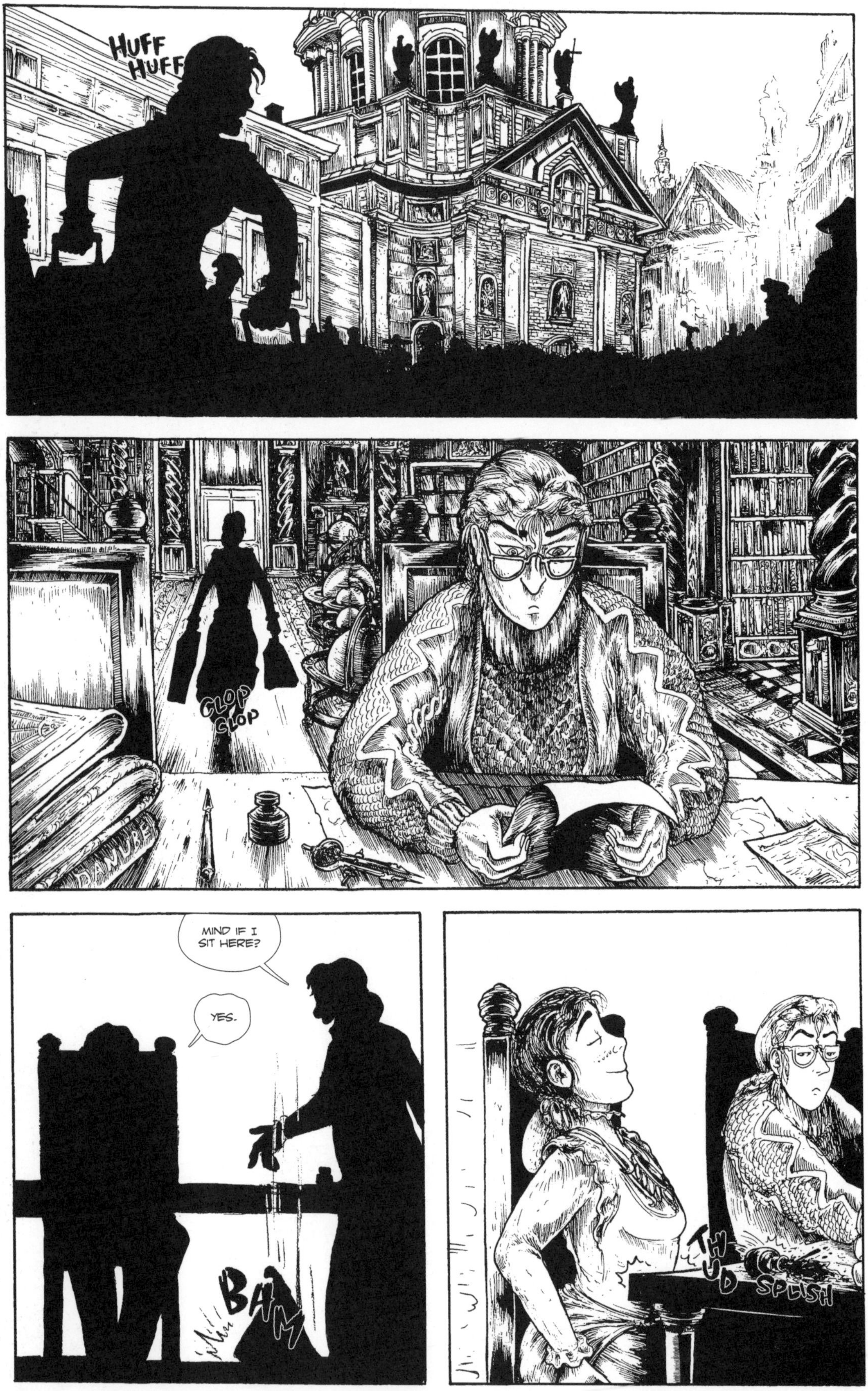
HUFF HUFF
CLOP CLOP
DANUBE
MIND IF I SIT HERE?
YES.
BAM
THUD
SPLISH

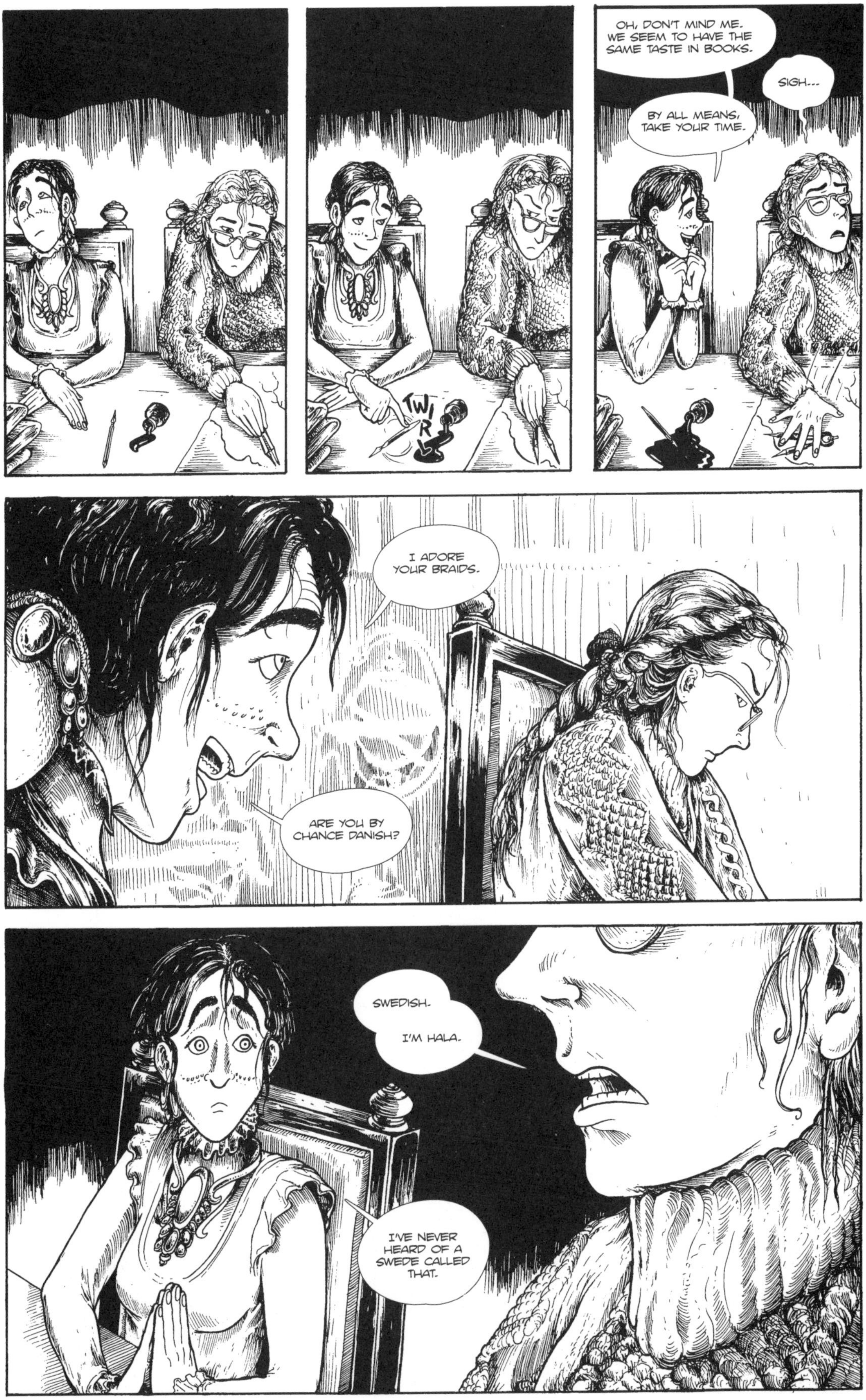
TWIRL
OH, DON'T MIND ME. WE SEEM TO HAVE THE SAME TASTE IN BOOKS.
BY ALL MEANS, TAKE YOUR TIME.
SIGH...
I ADORE YOUR BRAIDS.
ARE YOU BY CHANCE DANISH?
SWEDISH.
I'M HALA.
I'VE NEVER HEARD OF A SWEDE CALLED THAT.

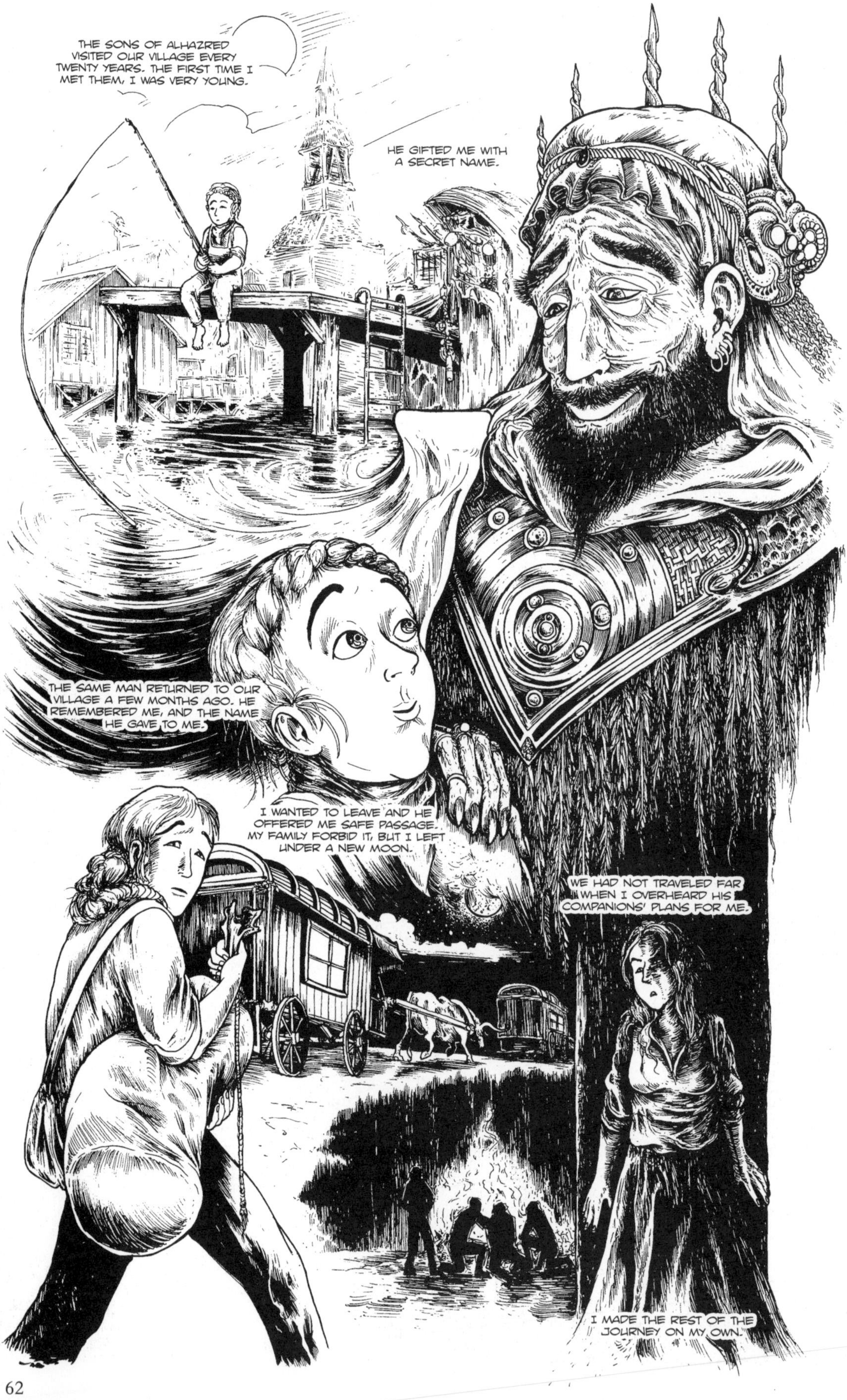
THE SONS OF ALHAZRED VISITED OUR VILLAGE EVERY TWENTY YEARS. THE FIRST TIME I MET THEM, I WAS VERY YOUNG.
HE GIFTED ME WITH A SECRET NAME.
THE SAME MAN RETURNED TO OUR VILLAGE A FEW MONTHS AGO. HE REMEMBERED ME, AND THE NAME HE GAVE TO ME.
I WANTED TO LEAVE AND HE OFFERED ME SAFE PASSAGE. MY FAMILY FORBID IT, BUT I LEFT UNDER A NEW MOON.
WE HAD NOT TRAVELED FAR WHEN I OVERHEARD HIS COMPANIONS' PLANS FOR ME.
I MADE THE REST OF THE JOURNEY ON MY OWN.

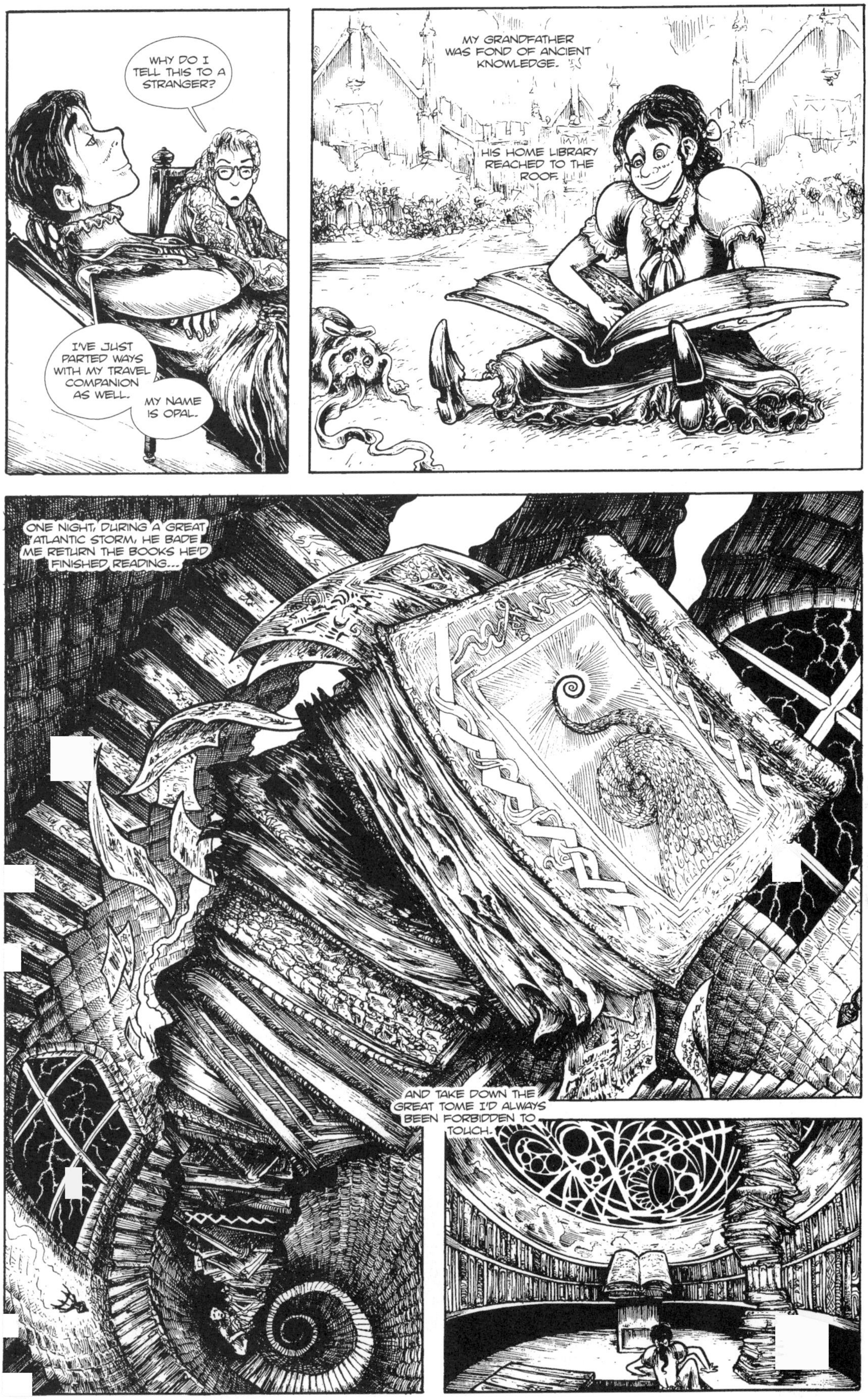
WHY DO I TELL THIS TO A STRANGER?
I'VE JUST PARTED WAYS WITH MY TRAVEL COMPANION AS WELL.
MY NAME IS OPAL.
MY GRANDFATHER WAS FOND OF ANCIENT KNOWLEDGE.
HIS HOME LIBRARY REACHED TO THE ROOF.
ONE NIGHT, DURING A GREAT ATLANTIC STORM, HE BADE ME RETURN THE BOOKS HE'D FINISHED READING...
AND TAKE DOWN THE GREAT TOME I'D ALWAYS BEEN FORBIDDEN TO TOUCH.

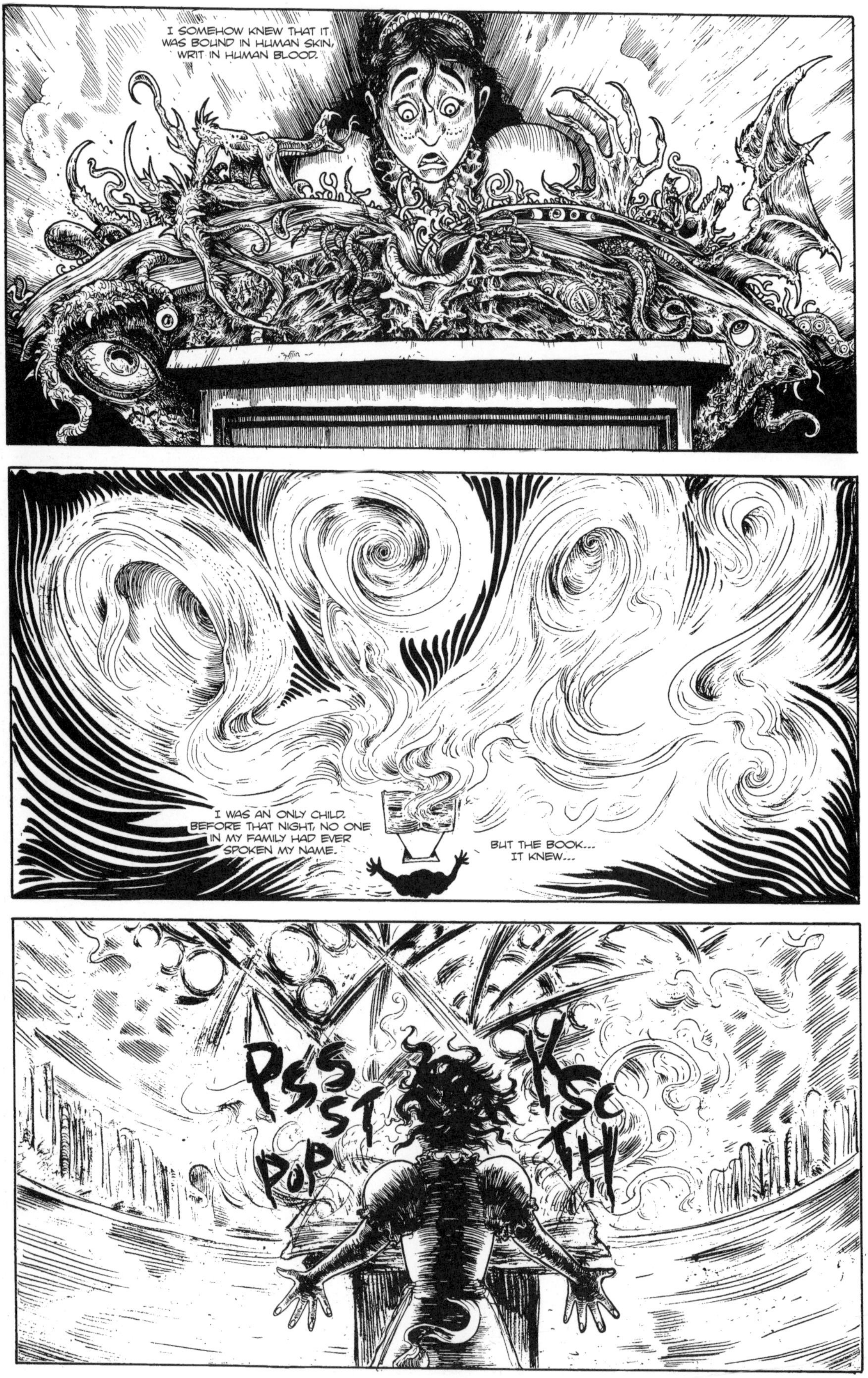
I SOMEHOW KNEW THAT IT WAS BOUND IN HUMAN SKIN, WRIT IN HUMAN BLOOD.
I WAS AN ONLY CHILD. BEFORE THAT NIGHT, NO ONE IN MY FAMILY HAD EVER SPOKEN MY NAME.
BUT THE BOOK... IT KNEW...
PSSST
POP
KSCTH

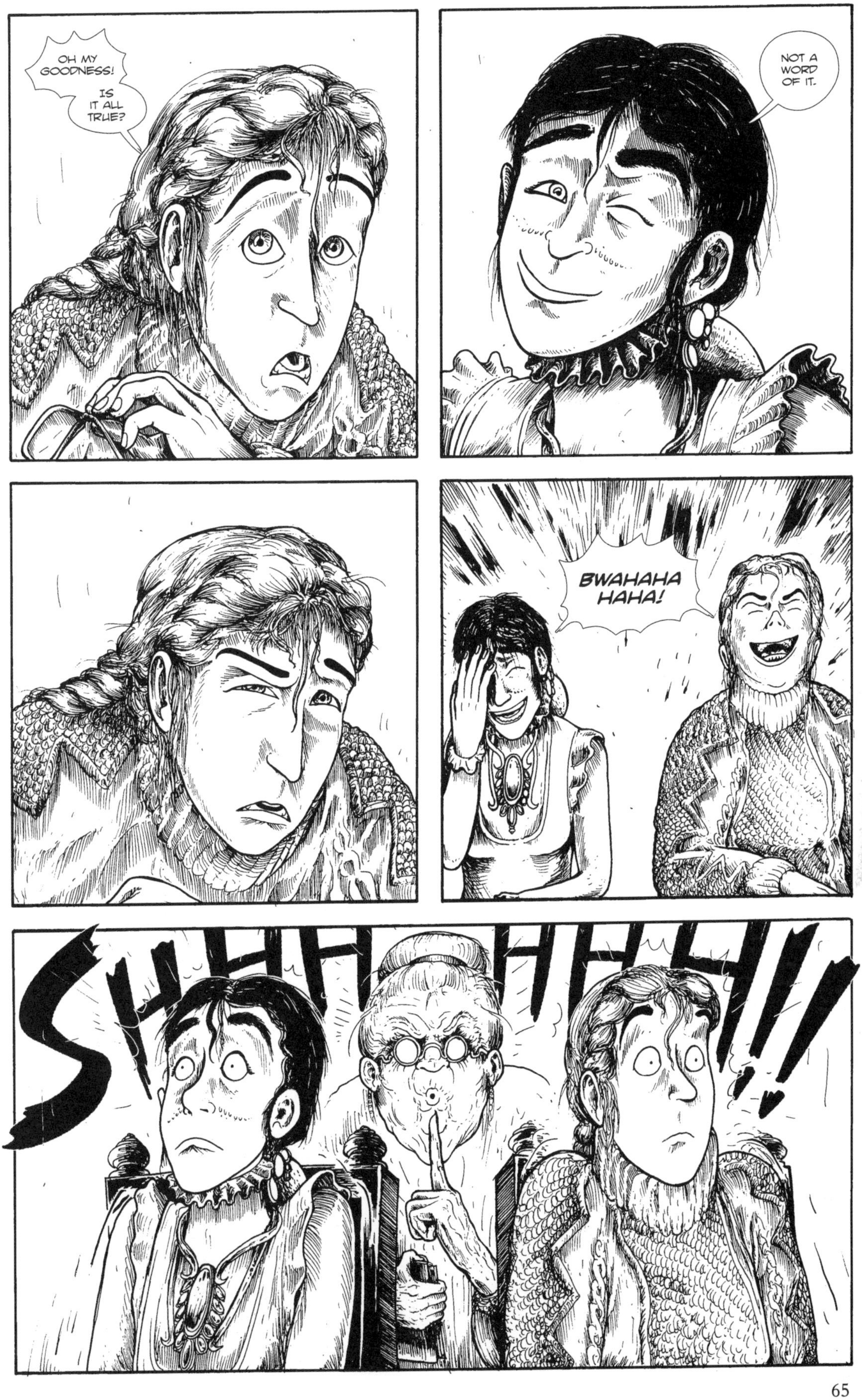
OH MY GOODNESS!
IS IT ALL TRUE?
NOT A WORD OF IT.
BWAHAHA HAHA!

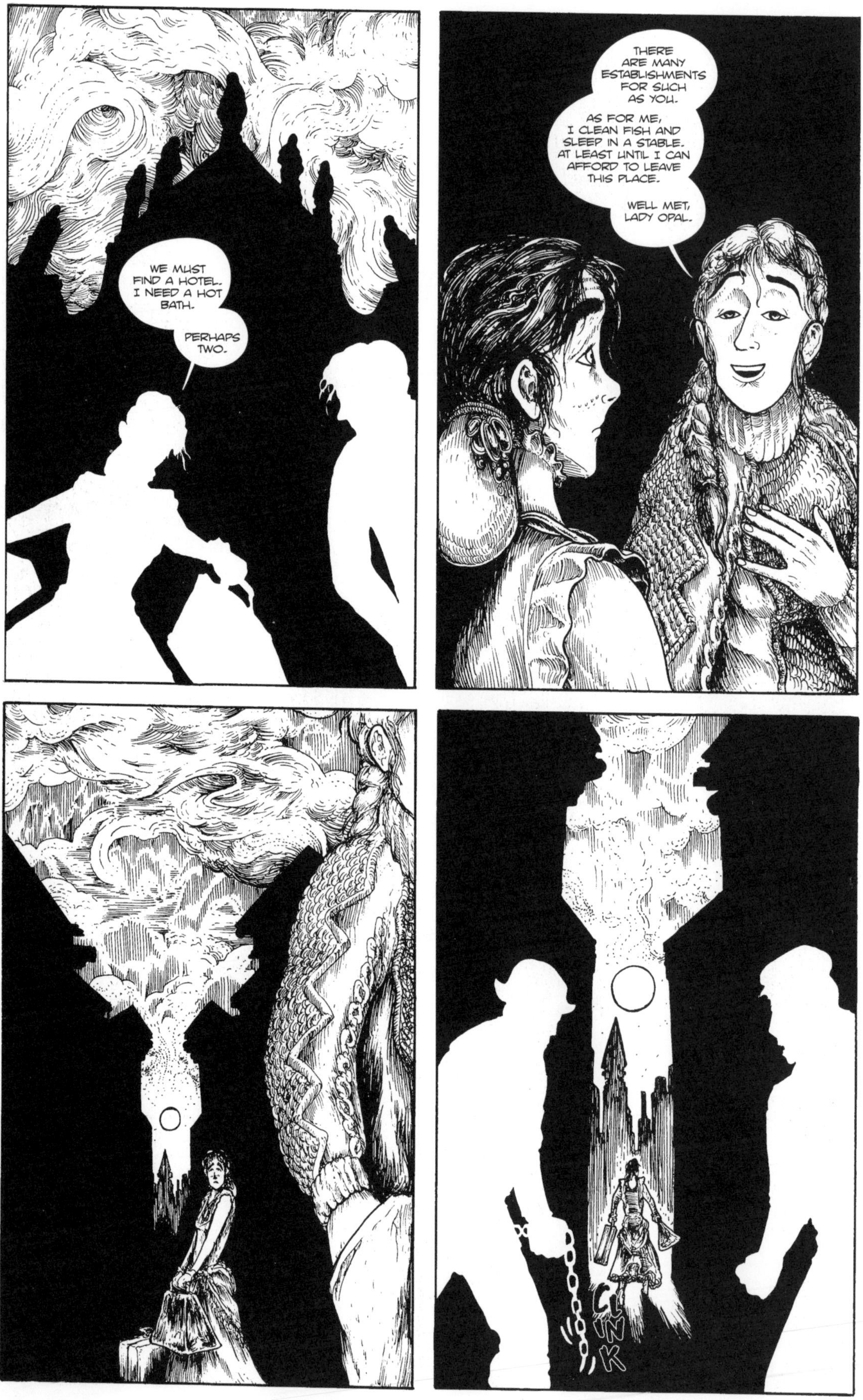

WE MUST FIND A HOTEL. I NEED A HOT BATH.
PERHAPS TWO.
THERE ARE MANY ESTABLISHMENTS FOR SUCH AS YOU.
AS FOR ME, I CLEAN FISH AND SLEEP IN A STABLE. AT LEAST UNTIL I CAN AFFORD TO LEAVE THIS PLACE.
WELL MET, LADY OPAL.
CLINK

CHNK
CHNK
HEH HEH
GASP!

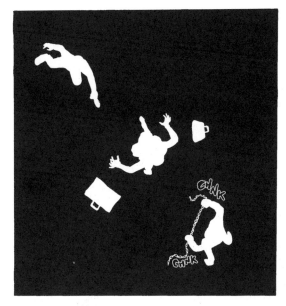

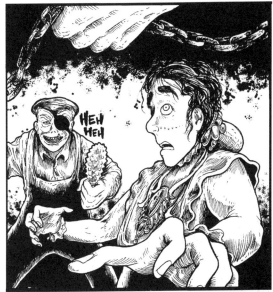

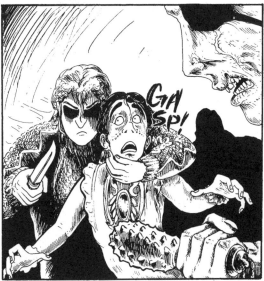

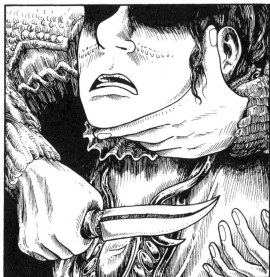

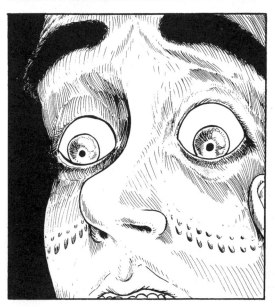

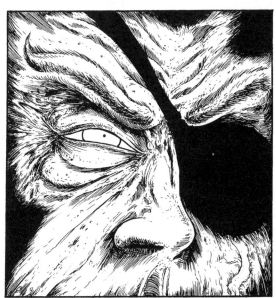

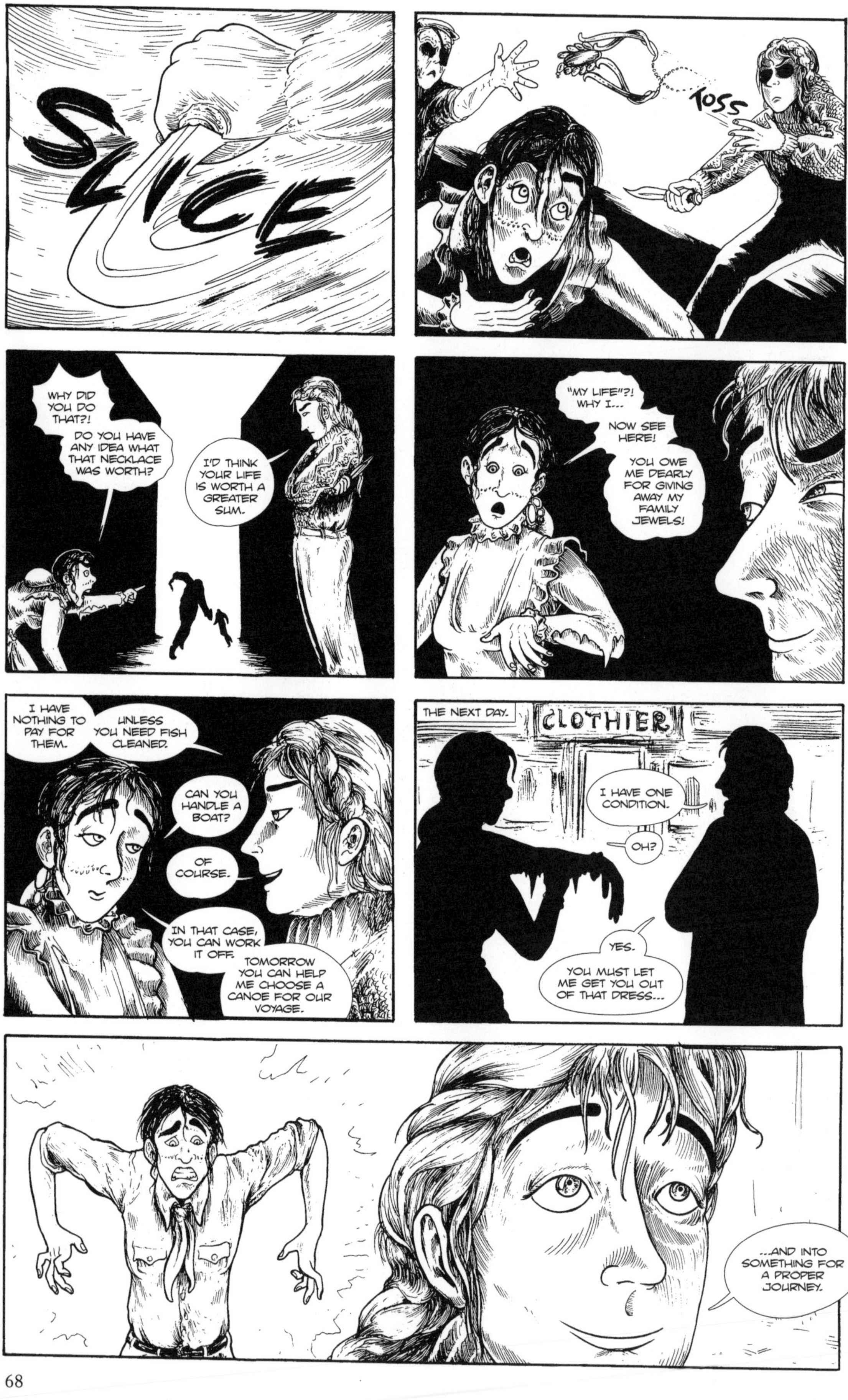

SLICE
TOSS
WHY DID YOU DO THAT?!
DO YOU HAVE ANY IDEA WHAT THAT NECKLACE WAS WORTH?
I'D THINK YOUR LIFE IS WORTH A GREATER SUM.
"MY LIFE"?! WHY I...
NOW SEE HERE!
YOU OWE ME DEARLY FOR GIVING AWAY MY FAMILY JEWELS!
I HAVE NOTHING TO PAY FOR THEM.
UNLESS YOU NEED FISH CLEANED.
CAN YOU HANDLE A BOAT?
OF COURSE.
IN THAT CASE, YOU CAN WORK IT OFF.
TOMORROW YOU CAN HELP ME CHOOSE A CANOE FOR OUR VOYAGE.
THE NEXT DAY.
CLOTHIER
I HAVE ONE CONDITION.
OH?
YES.
YOU MUST LET ME GET YOU OUT OF THAT DRESS...
...AND INTO SOMETHING FOR A PROPER JOURNEY.

I've always been interested in The Weird. The first people I blame for this fascination are my parents. Aside from being loveable misfits themselves, they went so far as to name my younger brother Merlin. I never stood a chance of being normal.

The first television I ever saw was Channel 49 in rural Indiana. 49 featured twenty-four hour a day programming of classic monster movies. It was black & white heaven. Before I could read, my corneas burned with images of Godzilla, Rodan, Gamera, (my personal favorite was Hedorah, aka The Smog Monster), Johnny Sokko & Giant Robot, and of course all the classic Universal monsters. Immediately thereafter came Sesame Street and Muppets, so I was relating to monsters before I ever tried to follow any human narratives.

By the time I was four we'd made the inevitable westward migration to the Grey Havens of rural mid-valley Oregon. That summer dad took me to see Star Wars in the theater. The story of a farm boy who happened to be a wizard/knight trapped in the middle of nowhere but destined for greatness resonated. The action figures and bubble gum cards ignited my fascination with collecting, which matured as I progressed from comic books to record albums.

The late seventies and early eighties now seem like a heyday for fantasy, but we were starved at the time. Any morsel of strangeness was something we savored. Whether it was Mork's first cameo appearance on Happy Days, the episode of Gilligan's Island wherein the castaways eat radioactive vegetables and gain superpowers, or that rerun of the Little Rascals with the infamous skeleton dance . . . everything out of the ordinary was grounds for conversation at recess the next day.

If anything brought out my inherent ability to tell stories of my own, though, it was Dungeons & Dragons. I already spent a great deal of time traipsing through the woods around our goat farm swinging a wooden sword. The closest mini-mart to hang around was three miles away over a steep hill. My imagination was my strongest weapon against boredom, and role-playing games offered a structure that inspired me on every level.

Thanks to Appendix N in the Dungeon Master's Guide and a hellion named Shane Tribble (I can't make this shit up) who lived a few fields away, it was not long before I discovered the writings of H.P. Lovecraft. The Call of Cthulhu RPG was, of course, the gate--we said every incantation one should not--and spent our sanity points with glee. By the time I was in high school, I covered my copy of HPL's Bloodcurdling Tales of Horror and the Macabre with the dust jacket from a math textbook, and whiled away many hours of in-school suspension exploring the Miskatonic and Dunwich.

Throughout my adolescence and adult life I exhausted Lovecraft's writings and his nearest circle. Robert E. Howard, Clark Ashton Smith, Ray Bradbury and the rest lived on my shelves. It didn't hurt that my mother was a librarian, or that my first job after I dropped out of college was at a bookstore. As a result, I was well versed in my King In Yellow decades before True Detective brought Robert W. Chambers' classic story cycle onto the best-seller list.

Algernon Blackwood was a name I came across fairly often, especially because Lovecraft spoke so highly of his work in the essay "Supernatural Horror in Literature." But somehow or other I had not taken time to read any Blackwood, even though I owned two copies of a hardcover collection, and of course "The Willows" was anthologized in David Hartwell's essential anthology, The Dark Descent.

It was only after I began writing and selling my own fiction around 2015 that I joined a reading group with several other published authors. The second story we tackled was "The Willows."

Needless to say, I got it on the first read. The foundation was built for me to appreciate everything Blackwood was doing with the language and atmosphere. Its place in the canon of weird fiction made perfect sense to me. It was a joy to finally read "The Willows" and take that trip down the Danube and share the wonder and awe of those two fools who thought they knew better than everyone who warned them along the way. I'd finally assimilated a classic gap in my knowledge, and then I moved on to the next reading assignment (Daphne Du Maurier's "The Birds").

Literally one week later, I was interviewing Jason Leivian for an article I was writing to celebrate the tenth anniversary of his nationally renowned Floating World Comics store. After I asked my questions and closed my notebook, he asked if I'd ever considered writing a comic. Of course I'd grown up a Marvel True Believer. My first book was Jack Kirby's Devil Dinosaur #1. And when Dark Horse sprouted up, I was the kid at the convention getting all their early titles autographed by the lonely creators who no one yet knew.

Jason asked me about writing because, in addition to publishing a number of short speculative fiction stories in anthologies and magazines, I'd just had my first standalone novella released, Starr Creek.

Before I began pitching ideas, Jason suggested adapting a classic from the public domain. "Something like Blackwood's 'The Willows,'" he said. I felt an immediate sense of synchronicity, having so freshly read that story. I am neither spiritual nor superstitious, but when coincidences like this arise, I tend not to ignore them. And within a week or so, I'd signed on to adapt "The Willows" into a graphic novel.

The first thing I made certain of was that I could collaborate with my friend Sam Ford. His illustration style was so far beyond what any first-time comic scriptwriter could hope for, and he had the chops, the background, and the desire. Sam had grown up on San Juan Island, apprenticed to award-winning comic artist Paul Chadwick. I'd read Chadwick's Concrete stories and books and was always impressed by the clean lines, and the realistic depiction of fantastic subjects.

Sam had done high caliber work for my bands: album covers, concert posters, t-shirts. But I knew he had the ability to do sequential work. We had just never been offered a project like this before. I was incredibly fortunate to be asked to write a novella by a publisher not long prior. This was the next invitation. We wouldn't have to shop the book around. We just needed to produce it. The fire was lit and we got cooking.

In rereading the original novella of "The Willows" with an eye toward adaptation into comic format, a few things became apparent. First off, there is an immense amount of descriptive detail that would need to be shown, rather than told. It was sixty pages of dense text from 1907, and required distillation down to 48 pages of images and word balloons. Sam and I both felt it was paramount to preserve the atmosphere and language of the original as much as possible. We had both seen so many of our favorite works turned into poor, watered-down, commercial dreck. We swore to honor the fans and make our Willows bulletproof to that sort of criticism.

What made a story great in 1907 is different from what readers in 2017 demand, though. And the prime area of dissonance in the case of "The Willows" was in regard to the characters. Back in Blackwood's day, depicting two colonial white male cyphers as marionettes that experience the strangeness on that sandbar was more than adequate. Lovecraft continued the tradition of dumping thin, wooden characters into immensely detailed settings and situations. That was par for the course in the early twentieth century. But it would not suffice for our modern needs.

If there were many character details to retain, we would have done so. But there were so few. We knew that the narrator was English, and his companion was "The Swede." Beyond that, their relationship made little sense. Supposedly these two had been on several journeys together, yet they seem to know each other almost not at all. If these men even had names, for crying out loud, we'd likely have kept them around.

Instead, we made a command decision to safeguard the story, and get creative with the characterization. How much richer might this tale become if the incidents happened to two people who had a relationship, back stories of their own, and--bear with me--names! And that's when the idea to make them women struck me.

As soon as I began to imagine the type of women who would have had the resources and agency to embark on a trek like this back in 1907, the ideas began to flow. Once Opal and Hala were born, the story quickly took shape.

The only other changes we made to the overall plot were minor fixes. The original ending was anticlimactic and a bit of a cop-out. So we opted for a more appropriately weird and mysterious ending, which seems to have been appreciated by every reviewer to date.

The other liberty we took simply had to do with reducing repetition. If we had gone for a straight adaptation of the text, Opal would have crawled in and out of her tent about thirty times. We reduced those superfluous actions for the sake of better storytelling. No regrets.

After the second issue of "The Willows" completed our story, we were sent photos of educators and students using our comics as study materials at several universities around the world. That was mind-blowing evidence that we had succeeded in what we set out to do, which was to take a 110-year-old story and make it relevant to today's readers, without selling out along the way.

Finally, it is my pleasure to offer our "Issue Zero" backstory of Opal and Hala's first meeting. I believe that reinforcing these characters takes nothing away from Blackwood, and adds depth to the story as we told it.

With luck, perhaps our heroines may find cause to go on a further round of original adventures one day. They certainly have the wits and resilience to get into further trouble.

Huge thanks to Jason Leivian for editing, publishing, and envisioning this project in the first place.

Thank you, Sam Ford, for being a true friend, for your beautiful, immaculate, and strange artwork, and for risking your sanity to meet our many deadlines.

And thank you, the reader, for dipping your paddle in the river, to turn over whichever adorable otter you inevitably find.

–Nathan Carson
June 2019

Nathan Carson
Name meaning: some Hebrew shit
Born Jun 23, 1973 (Cancer), Year of the
Water Ox.
Age -66 (in 1907)

Nathan Carson is a musician, writer, and
Moth StorySlam champion from Portland,
OR. He is widely known as co-founder and
drummer of the internationally touring
doom metal band Witch Mountain, host of
the XRAY FM radio show The Heavy Metal
Sewïng Cïrcle, and owner of the boutique
music booking agency Nanotear.

A regular on the weird fiction convention
circuit, he has published many short stories
and novelettes in critically acclaimed horror
anthologies. His first standalone novella
Starr Creek is out now. Read it.

www.nathancarson.rocks

Sam Ford
Name meaning: some biblical shit
Born Jan 5, 1987 (Capricorn), Year of the
Fire Rabbit.
Age -80 (in 1907)

Sam Ford is an acclaimed illustrator, and
drummer of the lightning-in-a-bottle
musical duo Wizard Rifle. Sam was
apprenticed as a youth to award-winning
comic book legend Paul Chadwick
(*Concrete*) and has used the skills he
learned to produce countless highly
detailed posters, album covers, and t-shirts
for bands as varied as Mountain Goats,
Agalloch, Pentagram, Black Cobra, and
Thrones.

He has called Portland, Los Angeles, and
New York City home, but is currently
based in Washington State, living a
hermetic life in a custom-built trailer,
cranking out comic books and music at a
fevered pace.

www.samfordcreations.com

Algernon Blackwood
Name Meaning: with whiskers, bearded
Born: Mar 14, 1869 (Pisces) Year of the Earth Snake
Age: 38 (in 1907)

Algernon Blackwood was one of the early twentieth century's preeminent writers of supernatural fiction. He was born into British aristocracy just outside London on 14 March, 1869. His father Sir Stevenson Arthur Blackwood was a devout Christian and Financial Secretary to the Postmaster General of England. Nonetheless, young Algernon discovered a variety of Eastern religions, philosophies, and mysticisms that corresponded more closely with his deep, lifelong identification with Nature.

Prone to dreaming and never a good student, Blackwood was removed from one school for stealing a book of poetry. His lone positive educational experience was a yearlong stint with the Moravian Brotherhood in the Black Forest of Germany. In that monastic environment he learned an asceticism that endured until the end of his life; he kept almost no personal effects and lived simply for one born to such an esteemed family.

As a teen, Blackwood considered life as a farmer, and embarked on a voyage to Canada, which he traversed by rail with his father. Later he operated a hotel there for a few months before moving to New York City where he found work as a reporter. Not long after, he became a writer for the New York Sun, and eventually the New York Times.

By his thirties, Blackwood had returned to England as an established author and began to pen the supernatural stories for which he is most famous. In June of 1900 he took a canoe trip down the flooded Danube River with his friend and literary collaborator Wilfrid Wilson (who, incidentally, was not Swedish). This journey--and a follow-up trip in 1905--inspired Blackwood's immortal novella "The Willows."

Blackwood lived a long life, fascinated by esoteric subjects, theosophy, spiritualism, and ghost stories. He was a member of the Hermetic Order of the Golden Dawn, and an enthusiastic outdoorsman. He wrote plays (the original Starlight Express), fifteen novels, a memoir, and an unknown number of short stories, articles, and essays. His adaptions of his own work were well received on radio, and he even appeared on the first ever television broadcast.

Ironically, Blackwood is largely remembered today due to the great reverence H.P. Lovecraft held for his writing, in particular "The Willows" which he deemed "the finest tale of supernatural horror ever written." Unfortunately the sentiment was not returned. Blackwood felt HPL's stuff was "sheer horror" and bereft of "cosmic wonder."

Never married, Blackwood was a loner who lived to be eighty-two, looking not unlike a healthier William S. Burroughs near the end. A quick search online will turn up videos of "Lock Your Door" and "The Reformation of St Jules" which he performed on camera in 1949, two years before he succumbed to a series of strokes, finally dying on Dec 10, 1951. His ashes were scattered in the Swiss Alps where he became one with the vast, natural forces whose omnipresence had always accorded with Blackwood's mystical temperament and so fascinated him in life.

Bio written by Nathan Carson, edited by Leigh Blackmore.